THE DEATH SHADOW RIDERS

Bank robber Jake Larribee saves Blaze Morgan from a cattleman's hanging. But then Blaze's handiness with his pistol lands them in deeper trouble. And whilst being beholden to a sutler and his daughter, they take on the biggest rancher in southern New Mexico, Simpson and his crew of the Slash Y ranch. Allied with three Mexican boys and their grandpappy, they begin a guerrilla war against the Slash Y — a war destined to end in one final bloodletting shoot-out.

ELLIOT CONWAY

THE DEATH SHADOW RIDERS

Complete and Unabridged

LINFORD
Leicester

First published in Great Britain in 2009 by
Robert Hale Limited
London

First Linford Edition
published 2010
by arrangement with
Robert Hale Limited
London

The moral right of the author has been asserted

British Library CIP Data

Conway, Elliot.
  The death shadow riders. - -
  (Linford western library)
  1. Western stories.
  2. Large type books.
  I. Title II. Series
  823.9'14–dc22

  ISBN 978–1–44480–203–0

Published by
F. A. Thorpe (Publishing)
Anstey, Leicestershire

Set by Words & Graphics Ltd.
Anstey, Leicestershire
Printed and bound in Great Britain by
T. J. International Ltd., Padstow, Cornwall

This book is printed on acid-free paper

To Debbie Bulley
for looking out for the old gringo
on his sojourns at St Hild's

1

The hammering on the door and the shout of, 'We know you're in there, Larribee! Are you comin' out peaceful like, or do we have to come in shootin'?' had a loudly cursing Jake Larribee, wearing only his well-patched red drawers and socks, rolling away from the girl in the bed with him and leaping to his feet.

More shouts and the rattling of the locked door hastened Larribee's departure from the Silver Sands bawdy house. He scooped up the rest of his clothes and gunbelt from the chair and, shielding his face as best as he could he hurled himself through the window.

He landed heavily, and painfully on all fours, his drawers and flesh slashed by the shattered glass and the sharp wooden splinters of the broken frame. Quickly he got back on to his feet and

1

in a high-foot lifting stride over the widely scattered pieces of glass, punctuated by curse words and gasps of pain, he made for the stairs that led from the veranda to the side alley, and his horse. He was hoping that there wasn't a sheriff's deputy waiting down there ready to grab him.

His hope was fulfilled, only his horse was standing there in the darkness. Although his hands were full with his gear Larribee leapt on his horse with the slickness of an Indian buck eager to ride out on a killing raid. He reached out and jerked the loosely hitched reins from the post and jabbed his stockinged feet into his horse's ribs, sending it pounding along into the deeper darkness of the town's back lots as shells from the lawmen firing at him from the cat house balcony passed close by him.

Larribee didn't ease back his horse until he had put fifteen minutes or so of hard riding between him and Silver Sands. Then reckoning that he had outrun any posse he rode his horse off the trail and into a thick stand of timber where he dismounted and put on his clothes.

Buckling on his gunbelt Larribee began to wonder how the law in Silver Sands had got on to him. He wasn't known, or so he had thought, as a road agent, a man with several wanted flyers posted on him, in this section of the Territory of New Mexico. He had done most of his stage and bank robbing as far north as the Texas Panhandle and Nevada border lands where things had become too hot for him with posses of marshals riding in his trail dust, so he had hard-assed it all this way south almost clear to the Mexican border, making sure to keep clear of the small shooting war going on between the Chisum and Murphy factions around Fort Sumner and Roswell.

Larribee knew that the Western Union wire service made it harder for men such as him who earned their keep outside the law to operate. In a matter of minutes a town sheriff could wire the descriptions of a bunch of desperadoes who had just robbed his town's bank to every sheriff in three counties whose town had a Western Union telegraph depot. And the bank raiders riding into some town, well away from the town in which they had raided the bank to spend the money, could be shot out of their saddles before they made it to the nearest bar.

Larribee cursed. It was sure becoming harder for a fella to earn a dishonest living.

Thinking realistically, Larribee didn't believe that a town's peace officer got up off his fat ass and prowled around his town with a fistful of Wanted flyers checking out the descriptions of any strangers in the saloons or cat house to see if they matched. No, he reasoned, as he swung back into his saddle, some man he had once ridden with must have seen him as he walked into the whorehouse and, being as hard up as he was, had fingered him for the reward money. Loyalty among owlhooters ran thin these hard times, Larribee thought glumly.

He decided that there was no sense worrying and wondering about something that had already happened. He had got clear, he thin-grinned, by the thickness of his drawers. His top priority was working out where did he go now? Did he cross the border and rob the bank of the first Mex town he rode to, if the town was big enough to boast a bank? Or did he scout around to try and find an honest sweat-raising job until things quietened down hereabouts?

Larribee didn't doubt that the telegraph wires would be humming with the news that Jake Larribee, bank robber, was here in the territory, so any chance he thought he had of sneaking into some town and rob its bank was gone. Every bank in the county would be posting extra guards on their front porches.

Riding along the main trail, even at night, was too risky. He could run into men hunting for him, so he would have to spend the rest of the night here in the trees. Then, come first light, ride along a side trail and see what came up. Which, when Larribee thought about it, was his normal way of living. At the dangerous trade he followed he couldn't plan his life more than the time it would take to pull off a successful bank heist and spend the takings. Though it had just been proved that he wasn't getting the time to spend what he was risking his neck for. A mournful-minded Larribee began to unsaddle his horse and make preparations for a cold, hungry night camp.

2

A bone-aching, heavy-eyed Larribee broke camp real early, following a little used trail he had picked up circling the trees. It headed south-west; where to, he would have to wait to find out. It ran away from Silver Sands which suited him.

He had watered Logan and fed him a hatful of grain. There was no need for his horse to go hungry; it wasn't Logan's fault he had missed out on a home-cooked breakfast and a few hours' sleep in a regular bed. And besides, he might have to call on Logan to high kick to get him out of trouble again. He was chewing on a mouthful of Logan's breakfast to ease his own hunger.

A few hundred yards ahead, Larribee saw that the trail curved round the edge of a split-face butte. The sun had come up fast and warm and Larribee felt alive once more. Ahead of him the trail was deserted and, looking over his shoulder at his back trail, it was likewise clear of any riders. Larribee's nerves relaxed somewhat and he sat easier in his saddle. He smiled. Roll on the next bank.

'Logan,' he said, 'we seem to be the only travellers on this trail. When we come across some water we'll stop for a short spell and I'll get me a fire goin' so I can have a cup of coffee to wash down those oats of yours. Which ain't the finest chow a man can break his fast with I can tell you.'

But Larribee unexpectedly discovered that he wasn't the only early traveller on the trail. Just round the edge of the bluff was a three-man camp with a fire going beneath a coffee pot.

The big man facing him, wearing a yellow duster, sprang to his feet. The wide-skirted coat flapped open and Larribee caught the glint of a lawman's badge pinned to the man's vest, and his right hand hovering over the butt of a belted pistol almost hidden by a bulging belly. Larribee nearly choked swallowing the last of the mashed up grain.

It was too late for him to haul Logan's head round and get to hell back around the butte fast and he sure wasn't loco enough to take on three men in a gunfight. He did some rapid thinking. He knew that he looked nothing like his printed likeness on the Wanted flyers. And the badge-wearing sons-of-bitches seemed to be making for Silver Sands so they wouldn't know about the near capture of the bank robber, Jake Larribee, in town. Unless they had picked up the news from the goddamn Western Union wire services, he thought, with some ill-feeling against everyone who worked for the company. He would have to bluff his way by them.

He gave the three a snake-oil drummer's smile and a forced, 'Howdee, gents,' keeping his hands well clear of his guns.

The big-bellied man favoured him with a narrow-eyed, taking-all-in gaze. 'You're a stranger in these parts, mister?' he growled, more as an accusation than a question.

Larribee began to sweat. One of the other lawmen had got to his feet. A smaller-built man sporting a straggling longhorn that reached below his chin. The Winchester he cradled was casually pointing in his direction. Larribee's grin stretched to his ears.

'I sure am, mister,' he replied. 'Just rode here from Fort Sumner seekin' ranch work that don't risk me gettin' a lump of lead in my hide.' His voice took on a plaintive whining tone. 'It was gettin' that a man couldn't tend his boss's cows without bein' set upon by the warrin' bully boys in the county!'

Larribee, with a great deal of relief, saw the small lawman's rifle swing away from him. 'Yeah, we've heard about the ruckus goin' on in Lincoln County,' brought further peace of mind to Larribee. His luck was still holding up.

Good sense told him not to push it any further, to say his farewells and continue on his way. He was just about to heel Logan in the ribs when he caught a clear sighting of the third man in the camp, a scowling-faced youngster. The shackles on his wrists told him he had been wrong thinking that he'd been another lawman. Then Larribee silently came out with a, 'Well, I'll be damned!' as he recognized the prisoner.

The last time he'd clapped eyes on Blaze Morgan had been in some dog dirt settlement on the southern rim of the Llana Estacado, drinking and whooping it up in the local gin palace with a bunch of other kids his age — kids who were rapidly making a name for themselves as hellraisers in the territory, going by the name of the 'Boys' and bossed over by William Bonney, a young desperado harbouring a killing streak. They were all double armed with shoulders draped with shellbelts. The death-dealing loads they were burdened with had them practically bow-legged. By what he had made out of their talk they had just pulled off a successful cattle-lifting raid and were blowing the proceeds in some style.

He later heard that they had hired their guns out to one of the factions in the Lincoln County trouble and now here was Blaze being brought in by the law. Larribee didn't owe Blaze anything and he opined that the kid didn't recollect seeing him in the saloon on the high plains, but he was curious to find out why Blaze had come south and what wrongdoing the law was bringing him in for.

'What's that young *pistolero* been up to, Sheriff,' he asked smiling. 'Robbin' some sodbuster's chicken coop?'

'Don't let that kid's sweet, altar boy's looks fool you, mister,' the big lawman replied. 'He shot dead a ranch straw boss in a saloon back there in Scottsburg. Me and Josh is takin' him to the county seat to stand trial for murder.'

'It weren't murder!' an angry-faced Blaze blurted out. 'It was self-defence! The crazy sonuvabitch threw down on me just because I bought this saloon girl a drink!'

The lawman cold-smiled at Blaze. 'That was the second mistake you made, bub, buyin' a drink for Burt Lee's bed partner. Your first mistake was goin' into the saloon when the XL crew were in there loosin' up somewhat before the big drive north in a coupla days' time.'

'I reckon that Burt could have drawn out his gun first, kid,' Josh said. 'Just as you say, Burt wasn't the most sociable of characters even when not whiskeyed up but everyone in the saloon says otherwise.'

Seing their foreman outgunned by a smooth-faced kid would have riled the XL ranch hands, brought blood into their eyes, Larribee thought. The only reason they hadn't shot down Blaze in retaliation there and then was the kid must have had them covered with his pistol and not one of them wanted to be the next man hitting the boards, dead. So they did the next best thing, branded him as a murderer and let the law put paid to him.

'But all the bastards were XL men!' Blaze cried, then let loose with a string of curses. 'I shoulda rode round that hog pen of a town,' he muttered, between his curse words.

'The way things turned out for you, kid, it would have been wiser to have kept on your horse,' Josh said. 'But you'll get your say in front of a judge and jury though I'll have to admit that with no one willin' to speak in your favour you could be taking that early mornin' walk to the hangin' post.'

Blaze, running out of curses, shot the lawman a drop-dead glare.

'If we had left you in the jail house back there in Scottsburg,' Josh continued, 'the XL crew would have hauled you out and strung you up on the handiest tree before Burt's body had got cold. Ain't that so, Phil?'

14

'Gospel true,' Phil said. 'Those cowhands would have had themselves a good old-fashioned lynchin' with the blessin's of their boss, Mr Saul Bentine.'

Larribee held no good feelings towards cattlemen, ranchers and crews. In his opinion they were an arrogant, stomping breed of men. They thought that they had the God-given right to drive their herds across sodbusters' hard-worked land seeking extra grass and water. They dealt out their own justice — Judge Lynch's law; a law that brooked no appeal. According to that law, Blaze, a longtime cattle and horse thief, was overdue for attending one of Judge Lynch's necktie parties. But not for the saloon shooting. One of the lawmen had said that the straw boss was a bully boy which fitted in with his jaundiced opinion of cattlemen in general. A man ought not to get strung up for defending himself.

The more Larribee thought about the raw deal Blaze was getting the angrier he became. He tried to tell himself that he had always been a loner and never interfered in any other fella's business. That way if he landed in trouble, like he did in Silver Sands, he had only himself to blame. Yet seeing the dejected-looking Blaze and the fearful fate the cattlemen's law had in store for him, gnawed at his guts, had him thinking of an action he never thought he would have to consider doing. He opined that he had done some foolish things in his life but what he was contemplating now could turn out to be the most crazy, and could get himself killed. So what, he thought, he could get that way robbing a bank.

'Well, *amigos*,' he said conversationally. 'Me and the kid oughta be on our way.'

A nervous smile flickered across Josh's face, wondering if he had heard right. He glanced across at Phil. He was showing the same, 'Did you hear that?' look. He switched his gaze back on to the drifter to ask him what the hell he meant and found himself eyeballing a drawn pistol. Josh swallowed hard. He had heard right.

'Now we don't want blood to be shed, mine or yours, do we, gents?' Larribee said. 'So just drop your rifle, Josh, and you, Phil, keep your hand away from your pistol.'

He heard Josh's rifle clatter on the ground and saw that the big lawman was making a point of keeping his hand clear of his pistol butt. 'Good,' he said. 'Once the kid's up on his horse we can leave you to enjoy your coffee.'

He gave them both a hard-eyed look, before saying, 'Now you're maybe harbouring thoughts that bein' there's only one of me and two of you all riled up at bein' thrown down by a ragged-assed drifter, you might take the chance and go for your guns. If you think that a kid who shot a man in self-defence is worth that risk then go ahead and make your play. If one of you is alive after the shootin' you can tell whoever it is who finds you that you tried to outshoot the bank robber, Jake Larribee.'

In all his bank-heisting days, Larribee, though he had winged more than a few men, he had never put a man down for good but he hoped that the 'Dead or Alive', on the Wanted flyers posted on him would cause the two lawmen to think deeply about taking him on.

Neither of the lawmen so much as twitched a finger; his grandstanding talk seemed to have paid off. He kept his relief from showing in his face.

Phil's nervous gaze fixed on the steady as a rock pistol held in the hand of the notorious owlhoot, Jake Larribee. Though Larribee had done most of his robbing north of Fort Sumner he had seen the flyers posted on him and figured that a bad-ass who could walk into a bank and rob it wouldn't give a spit if he was forced to gun down him and Josh. He had to clear his throat before he could speak. 'Get the shackles off the kid, Josh,' he ordered. 'We ain't seekin' trouble with you, Mr Larribee.'

Josh took the key out of his pocket and walked across to Blaze.

'Don't just sit on your ass, boy; oblige the gent and get on to your feet!' Larribee growled. 'Then mount up, pronto; we ain't got all day to hang about here.'

A gaped-mouthed Blaze leapt to his feet, hands outstretched for Josh to free them. He still hadn't taken it in that he'd been saved from a hanging. Though, by the time he had gathered up his rifle and gunbelt and swung into his saddle he was broad-grinning at his saviour.

'I'm ready to ride, Mr Larribee!' he called out.

'There's another job to do before we ride out, kid,' Larribee replied. 'These two gents are goin' to do us one more favour. They're goin' to heave their guns into yonder crick. Then they won't be tempted to back-shoot us as we pull away.'

There came a flurry of movement by

Josh and Phil and Larribee heard the sound of several splashes in the water. He gave a genuine smile this time round.

'You've been mighty obligin', gents,' he said, then shouted across at Blaze. 'OK, kid, let's make tracks so these lawmen can eat their chow!'

In a spray of hoof kicked-up dust and stones the pair rode out.

'Where we headin' for, Mr Larribee?' Blaze asked as he caught up with him.

Larribee cast a sidelong sour-faced look. 'I came south to get outa trouble, kid. I ain't been in this part of the territory more than a few hours and I've had a coupla run-ins with the law already. I'm headin' for Arizona where I ain't known as a bank robber. You can go where you fancy.'

Blaze knew that he was the cause of one of Mr Larribee's brushes with the law, but seeing the off-putting look he was getting he declined to ask him what the other trouble with the law was. One thing was for sure, he was beholden to

Larribee. To pay off that debt he would have to ride with the unsociable old fart, if it was OK with him.

'I ain't got any particular place in mind, Mr Larribee,' he replied, 'except to get to hell outa New Mexico. I'd like to tag along with you apiece until we ride into some town that suits me.'

Larribee twisted ass in his saddle until he was almost looking directly in Blaze's face. Blaze reckoned he was seeing Mr Larribee the way the bank tellers saw him before they handed him the bank's takings. He wished now he hadn't asked the question.

'You can ride with me, kid, for a spell,' Larribee said, as he straightened up in his saddle. 'But me and Logan here, ain't partial to riding with blabbermouths, OK?'

'That suits me fine, Mr Larribee,' replied Blaze. He gave a bleak smile. 'Thinkin' that I was due to be dancin' on the end of a rope in a few days' time has kinda dampened the need to gab outa me for the time bein'.'

'Yeah, I can see how that situation could upset a fella,' Larribee said. 'Now let's get some speed on and get across the Arizona line, wherever that is, before we have any more trouble with the law.'

3

After they had forded the Rio Grande, Larribee and Blaze found out from a Mexican sheepherder that it would be at least three days' hard riding before they made it to the Arizona border. Being that neither of them carried any supplies it would also be a hungry one, likewise for the horses. The small bag of grain Larribee had for Logan would hardly stretch to feeding Blaze's mount. And he couldn't see Logan willingly share his feed with another horse. He would be ornery enough to sit on his butt and refuse to move.

The horses, he knew, could turn out to be his and the kid's neck savers and had to be fed. That meant stopping at the first town, settlement, farm, whatever, to buy some grain and, if possible, rations for him and Blaze. Which went against the urgency to shake the dust of the Territory of New Mexico off Logan's hoofs as fast as he could.

Larribee cursed silently. He was beginning to think that riding south was like jumping from the griddle-iron into the goddamned fire. He did some more cursing, on the heads of the eastern owners of the banks he had robbed, who, being so put out at him taking their money, had put a dead-or-alive bounty on his head. Bank robbing, Larribee, told himself, wasn't a hanging offence, unless tellers were killed during a holdup. The sons-of-bitches were dishing out cattlemen's law. He ceased his silent ranting and, looking across at Blaze, told him of his decision to try and get feed for the horses and supplies for themselves.

'But if those Western Union bastards have run a wire into the town we ride on and chew on our gunbelts to ease our cravin' for chow, *comprende?*'

'*Comprende*, Mr Larribee,' replied Blaze, opining that going hungry was a damn sight better option than dancing at the end of a hanging rope. He thought that Mr Larribee was worrying too much. He couldn't see the law west of the Rio Grande putting themselves out to rope in a penny-ante bank robber. By what he'd heard in this stretch of territory the sheriffs and marshals had a whole army of bad-ass *pistoleros* to contend with; as far as he was concerned he'd broken no law killing a man in a fair fight. And they were riding further away from the vengeance seekers at the XL.

★ ★ ★

Late afternoon on the second day just when Larribee was beginning to wonder if they would ever come across so much as a shack in this desert of a land he saw a cluster of buildings shimmering in the fierce heat-haze ahead of them.

'I ain't seein' things am I, kid? he croaked.'

'No, you ain't, Mr Larribee,' Blaze said. He stood up in his stirrups and

25

narrow-eyed the buildings. 'Though it don't seem a place of great size. And I don't see a line of Western Union poles leadin' to it.'

Larribee grunted and flashed Blaze a suspicious, beady-eyed glance, but Blaze hid his smile well. 'Good,' he said. 'M'be we'll be able to have a home-cooked meal sitting at a table.'

Amos Brewster, owner of the Sutler's store in the settlement of San Remo, stacking boxes of supplies on the loading bay, saw the two riders coming in. He stopped what he was doing and walked back into his store. When coming out again he was carrying a double-barrelled shotgun. He leaned it up against a crate then, grim-faced, he eagle-eyed the closing-in riders.

Brewster knew that it wasn't good business acumen to greet two potential customers cradling a shotgun but then again it wasn't wise to welcome two men he couldn't recognize with a wide smile and welcoming arms until he had assessed them and knew what their business in San Remo was. Here in the South-west there were Comanche trails, Apache trails, cattle trails, all shown on maps, and one that wasn't shown on any map, the outlaw trail, passing close by San Remo.

Brewster was a worried man. Not for the first time he cursed his stubbornness in not pulling up stakes and setting up business elsewhere. It was not that he had such a thriving business here in San Remo and he had an added, bigger worry: a daughter, coming up to sixteen, who was blessed with the dark-eyed Mexican beauty of her late, and much lamented, mother.

Until now, with the threat of the shotgun, he had managed to keep the horn-dog ranch-hands of the Slash Y at bay when they came into San Remo on their monthly payday whoop-up. It was hardly worth all the hassle for the little trade in supplies he got from Lafe Simpson, the boss of the Slash Y. Then there were the men who frequented the outlaw trail. Bully boys who took what they desired — gold, liquor, women — by the gun. So there it was, he thought bitterly, cursed with a daughter as stubborn as he was who wouldn't leave San Remo without him. Brewster switched his full attention onto the two strangers again.

One of them, he observed, didn't look much older than his daughter, Carla, which didn't mean anything. He'd heard tell of a gang of kids around Fort Sumner and Roswell who were involved in a real shooting war. The older rider, lean-framed, had the every which way gaze of a man with the law riding close behind him. Yet Brewster had to admit that neither of them had the hungry, wolf-like looks of hard-bitten desperados.

Larribee and Blaze drew up their horses in front of the store, Larribee smiling a greeting.

'We'd like to buy some feed for our horses, mister,' he said. 'And we're wonderin' if there's a *cantina* or an eatin'-house here. We ain't eaten for a coupla days bein' that our goddamned mule took off while we were asleep with all our rations on its back.'

That was as good a lie as he'd ever heard spun, Brewster thought. Mules, he knew, were cantankerous critters, but even when spooked they tended not to travel far. And besides, the mule would have left tracks clear enough for the tall lying bastard and his angel-faced partner to follow. He was definitely right about the pair of strangers being a couple of jumps ahead of some sheriff's posse. But trade was trade and he wasn't prosperous enough to pick and chose his customers.

'There isn't an eating-house in San Remo,' he said. 'The building next door is the *cantina* but Burgess, the owner, don't serve meals. He'll supply you with rotgut moonshine or a Mex woman.' Feeling the need to unburden his depressing thoughts about his failing business to anyone who would listen, he said, part-smiling, 'As you can see, gents, there isn't much of San Remo left. I'm barely getting by with the supplies I sell to the Slash Y and the few Mex dirt farmers still working their land just outside town. The shack across the way is Seth Johnson's place. As well as being the barber Seth is the nearest to a doc we have in San Remo. When the Slash Y crew come into town on paydays Seth is real busy cleaning up the bullet and stab wounds the *loco* sonsuvbitches inflict on themselves when liquored up. The other buildings you can see are boarded up; the owners went bust! The town ain't rich enough to afford a sheriff.' Brewster gave a twist of a smile. 'No doubt you gents have troubles of your own to contend with without listening to mine. If you step down I'll weigh you out what measure of grain you want and I'll ask my daughter to rustle you up some hot food. There's water round the back if you want to see to your horses.'

Larribee didn't give a hoot if a twister blew away what was left of this dump of a town. He was highly pleased to hear that San Remo had no legal badge-toting officer of the law. That meant if trouble showed up it would come from only one direction, along the trail they had used, a trail he would keep a watchful eye on as he enjoyed a home-cooked meal.

'*Muchas gracias*,' he said, and both of them dismounted and led their mounts to the rear of the store.

They had fed and watered the horses and loose-hitched them to the rail in front of the store, enabling them to win a few precious seconds if they spotted the dust of fast-moving riders along their back trail.

They were now sitting at a table near one of the windows. The table was covered with a clean white cloth with eating irons laid on it. Larribee, trying not to make it too obvious to the sutler who was busy behind the store counter, kept casting sidelong glances out of the window. His mouth watered with the smell of frying steaks and brewing coffee.

Blaze was not only looking forward to the meal but eager to see the sutler's daughter. He didn't think she'd match up to the black-haired, flashing-eyed Mexican *señoritas* him and the boys had sparked up to at Fort Sumner. He grinned to himself. But she ought to be easier on the eye than the po-faced Mr Larribee was.

Larribee noticed that Blaze still had his hat on. He leaned across the table and hissed angrily, 'Take off your hat, kid! You ain't sittin' in some ranch cookhouse waitin' to be dished out with a mess of beans! The girl's made some effort, laid out the table real nice. Try to show her that we ain't a coupla backwoods hicks!'

Blaze, with a lowered-eyed gaze and a muttered, 'OK,' removed his hat, and Larribee saw how he had came by the name Blaze — his thick, black hair was marked by a wide grey streak.

'Now you know why I keep my hat on, Mr Larribee,' Blaze said on seeing his surprised look. 'A Comanche war band hit the wagon train I was with just as it was crossing the Red heading for New Mexico. The sonsuvbitches butchered my pa and ma and kid sister and every other living soul with the wagons. If my pa hadn't pushed me in a patch of reeds and told me to keep quiet and not move I would have been killed. It was two days before a Texas Ranger patrol found me. I was only four years old at the time.' Blaze touched the grey streak. 'This kinda grew with me.'

Larribee felt more sympathetic towards Blaze. What the kid had gone through would have sent a a preacher man riding on the wild side, to live, or die, fast and furiously. He would have to ask him why he had parted from Billy the Kid and the rest of his gang, though not now; the kid had bared his soul enough already.

Larribee heard Blaze give a low whistle and swung round in his chair and saw the girl carrying two plates of food. Larribee took women, when he wanted them, as they came, fat, thin, comely-looking or plain, downright ugly, but the young, proud-breasted girl whose long raven-black hair was held back from her high-boned face by a silver comb had him gaping as though he was as young and wild as Blaze.

A shy-eyed Carla set the plates down on the table. 'Enjoy your meal, *señors*,' she said soft-voiced. 'I will bring you your coffee as soon as it is ready.' With a swirl of her skirt she turned and hurried back into the kitchen.

Larribee grinned, Blaze had rammed his hat back on. Seeing Blaze's admiring, wide-eyed look, his grin turned into a scowl.

'Messin' about with a female would've got you strung up if I hadn't been passin' by,' he grated. 'That sutler's got a shotgun handily placed and he'll use it if he sees you foolin' around with his daughter and I don't want to catch any of the shot in my hide. Eat your steak then we can get on our way to Arizona.'

Blaze could see Larribee's point and not wanting to get on the wrong side of a man who had saved his life, picked up his knife and fork and cut at his steak, consoling himself with the blood-stirring thought that he'd meet other girls in Arizona and would be able to spend more time with them once he'd parted company with Larribee. But still, he reckoned, the sutler's daughter was a real beauty. Even the old goat, Mr Larribee, had gawped at her.

★ ★ ★

Larribee was sitting back relaxed in his chair. He'd eaten well and was on his second cup of coffee, a welcome change to the stewed, thick brew he was used to drinking. And no bunch of riders were rib-kicking their mounts along the San Remo trail. He saw Blaze push back his chair and get to his feet and flashed him a fish-eyed look.

'I'm only goin' to the crapper, Mr Larribee,' Blaze said tetchily. 'My bladder's bustin'! I've gotta go.'

'Yeah, OK, then,' replied Larribee.

Again he favoured Blaze with another withering glare. 'If I so much as hear you pass the time of day with that girl I'll come out and pistol-whip you and haul you outa town laid out across your horse's ass, *comprende*, boy?'

'Yeah, I understand,' a scowling-faced Blaze answered, thinking that he'd never seen a more worrying man before. He wondered why the old bastard's hair hadn't turned white like his as he walked out of the store.

Carla, helping her father to check the Slash Y supplies at the front of the store, heard the rattle of wagon wheels. She looked up sharply; there were two outriders with the wagon. She gave a gasp of fear as she recognized the bulkier of the two escorts, Bull Drummond, the ranch foreman.

Brewster heard his daughter's frightened cry and came up alongside her. He put a reassuring hand on her shoulder. 'You go inside, girl, and stay there,' he said. 'I'll see that the wagon's loaded as fast as I can.' He watched his daughter run inside then, grim-faced, he turned and eyeballed the wagon and the riders coming up to the store. If that big barrel of lard, Bull Drummond, attempted to put his dirty paws on Carla again, he vowed, he'd blow lumps off him with his shotgun and to hell with the risk of being gunned down by the other two Slash Y men.

'Your supplies are ready to be loaded on the flatbed, Drummond,' he said, before the dust raised by the wagon as it drew up in front of the store, had settled. He edged a little closer to the shotgun.

'Help Jack to load up, Billy,' Bull said, as he dismounted. 'I'm about to pay a call on that purty gal I saw goin' back inside.' He grinned lewdly. 'M'be I'll be able to sweet-talk her into comin' and have a drink with me in Casey's.'

Bull stepped up on to the porch, his great bulk overwhelming Brewster, but the sutler stood his ground. Carla was all the family he had left in the world and her well-being came before anything else — the store, his life.

'You help your men to load the wagon, Drummond,' he said, as firm-voiced as he could. 'I don't want you pestering my daughter.'

In spite of all the fat he was carrying, Bull could move fast. Snarling, he brought his right hand round and dealt Amos a vicious blow on the side of the jaw that sent the sutler crashing to the floor with a sharp cry of pain. Carla, hearing the ominous thud, came dashing out of the store her eyes wide with fear. A broad-grinning Bull grabbed her by the waist and pulled her to him. Carla felt the the stickiness of her molester's throat-gagging body sweat through the thinness of her clothes. Screaming, arms and legs lashing out, she struggled frantically to get out of his vice-like grip.

After relieving himself, Blaze took it in his head to stroll round to the front of the store to thank the girl for the fine meal she had dished up. The grumpy old bastard, Larribee, couldn't find fault with him for that, it was he who had told him to take off his hat and act like a gent. The girl's scream had him breaking into a run, pistol drawn. He turned the corner of the building and, in a split-second, he took in the scene: the sutler lying in a heap on the porch, the girl struggling in the arms of a big bear of a man. An angry-faced Blaze brought up his pistol and pulled off one shot.

Bull gave out a howl of pain and let go of Carla to clutch at his shattered left shoulder. Mad-eyed with pain and rage he looked at the blood seeping through his fingers then glared at Blaze. Dirty-mouthing and roaring he made a grab for his pistol with his good hand. Without any hesitation Blaze fired a second load that put a red-rimmed hole in the centre of Bull's forehead, silencing his roars forever. Bull staggered back on his heels swaying unsteadily for a moment or two before slipping off the edge of the porch to raise the dust several inches as he hit the ground.

Blaze, eyes on the girl now kneeling at her father's side, gave an involuntary twitch at the sound of another shot. He looked across at the wagon just in time to see the second rider slump over his saddle horn and then Larribee came out of the store holding a smoking pistol loosely on the wagon driver.

'You ain't about to join in the shootin'?' Larribee said, hard-voiced.

'Not me,' replied the driver, a grey-chinned old man. 'I'm only paid to drive this wagon and help out the cook. But I can't speak for Mr Simpson, my boss. I figure that he'll be more than a mite upset when he hears that his straw boss has been killed and one of his top hands sorely wounded by the look of him. More than likely he'll want a few words with you.' The old man gave a gapped-toothed smile. 'With a bunch of armed men to back him up.'

'Yeah, well, that's m'be so,' Larribee said. 'But you tell him that me and the boy didn't start this business.' Which he knew would be a waste of words. He and the kid had poked a stick in the eyes of the owners of two spreads now — stomping men who always got even. Larribee cold-smiled. They had to quit New Mexico soon or the kid would be likely to shoot down every straw boss in the territory.

He was about to tell Blaze to help the girl with her pa but he was already helping the sutler to get on to his feet. Blaze glanced at him.

'It weren't my doin', Mr Larribee, honestly,' he said. 'He was goin' to do the girl harm.'

'Yeah, I know,' Larribee said. 'I was all set to plug the sonuvabitch myself, but you beat me to the draw. Don't fret none, it was a righteous killin'. Help the girl to see to her pa. I'll see to the loadin' of the wagon.' And with an item of freight the old mule skinner didn't expect to be hauling, he thought. 'Then we'll get to hell out of this territory before we raise any more trouble for ourselves.'

'I want to thank you both for coming to our aid,' Amos Brewster said. 'That swine, Bull Drummond, he was the Slash Y straw boss, couldn't keep his filthy paws off Carla.' He forced a painful grimace of a smile. 'And he didn't do me any good either.'

The ashen-faced sutler was sitting on a chair at the rear of the store with an anxious-looking Carla at his side with a comforting arm around his shoulder.

'We're sorry things got outa hand, Mr Brewster,' Larribee said. 'But those two sons — beggin' your pardon, missee, those fellas chose to make a fight of it.'

'Now you've got to think of yourselves by riding out of San Remo,' Brewster said. 'Before Simpson, boss of the Slash Y, and his wild crew come looking for you.'

'How much of a lead will we have on those wild boys?' Larribee asked. 'Bein' that that old man had his team feelin' the whip before the wagon had rolled its own length. How far is it to the Slash Y?'

'Six miles or so,' replied the sutler. 'Simpson will have to round up some of his boys, that'll take time. And then he could be making one of his regular business trips to Mr Bentine who owns the XL spread east of here. And now the Slash Y have just lost their straw boss the crew won't dare to leave their ranch duties to set up a hunt without their boss's sayso. That ought to win you enough time to get you well on the way to where you're heading for. But don't bank on all those ifs: get ridin' now!'

In spite of his grogginess Brewster didn't miss the brief exchange of glances between the two drifters and guessed that somewhere along their back trail they'd had a run in with the XL and felt bold enough to ask if it was so.

'Have you had some trouble with Saul Bentine?' he said.

Brewster noticed that his question

had the pair again passing significant glances between them.

'Well, er, not exactly with Bentine,' Larribee said. 'But Blaze here shot dead his straw boss.'

Brewster jerked upright in the chair, a sudden movement that caused him to wince with pain. 'Gunned down Burt Lee. Well, I'll be damned!' he gasped and gave an eyebrow-raised look at Blaze. His daughter did likewise.

Blaze saw their looks and it embarrassed him somewhat. 'I was forced to plug him,' he said defensively. 'Ain't that so, Mr Larribee?' He favoured Larribee with an appealing-eyed look. He didn't want the girl to think that he was a trigger-happy *pistolero* shooting down men as the mood took him.

'Blaze is right,' Larribee replied. 'Like that fella who had his paws on your daughter he drew his gun on the boy and he was forced to defend himself.'

'Whatever way it happened,' a worried-faced Brewster said, 'it's long past the time both of you were headin'

44

towards where you're bound for. Bentine and Simpson aren't forgivin' men. Carla, rustle up some rations for them, quickly. You give her a hand, Blaze, you'll know what you're short of.'

Blaze didn't need any second asking; in a flash he followed Carla into the storeroom.

In spite of the mule still kicking away in his head, Brewster grinned at Larribee. 'The boy put his life on the line to save Carla from that sonuvabitch,' he said. 'I figure he's entitled to pass a few words with her, boy-girl fashion.'

Larribee grinned back. 'He'll appreciate it,' he said. 'The last few hours for him ain't been joyful. A while back I saved him from bein' strung up on account of him shootin' that straw boss and then he's had to yank out his pistol again. Yeah, I reckon he'll look kindly on you for allowin' him to be in your daughter's company.'

'It won't be for long though,'

Brewster said. 'I'll be more at peace with myself seeing your trail dust headin' towards Arizona, or wherever you're bound for. And that's meant in no disrespect, Mr Larribee.'

'No offence taken, Mr Brewster,' Larribee said. 'No one will be more happy than yours truly when I'm clear of New Mexico.' He raised his voice. 'Time we were movin' out, kid! Unless you want to do some more killin'.'

* * *

Brewster stood alongside his daughter on the store's porch watching Larribee and Blaze ride out. He heard Carla's soft-voiced, but fervent, 'Vaya con Dios!' and he had the ugly thought that if Bentine and Simpson caught up with them they would be beyond the help of any god.

At a steady, ground-eating lope they cleared the last of the outlying shacks of San Remo when Larribee turned suddenly in his saddle and frosty-eyed Blaze.

'When you start a gunfight, boy,' he said, 'make sure you're the one that ends it!'

'How's that, Mr Larribee?' a puzzled Blaze asked, his thoughts on the few minutes he had spent close to the sweet-smiling Carla abruptly ended.

'That fella I winged,' continued Larribee, 'was about to draw a bead on you while you were occupied with the girl and her pa.' He shook his head. 'You young so-called *pistoleros* won't see old age that's for sure. And that goes double for your one time *amigo*, William Bonney. Now let's get these horses' legs stretched.'

Blaze, though angry at Larribee's down-putting of the 'Boys' held his peace. Old goat or not, deep inside him he knew that Mr Larribee was speaking the truth. The Boys were running wild all over Roswell and Fort Sumner, but one day their luck would run out. Mr Larribee seemed an *hombre* who would try and keep the edge in any hairy situation he found himself in, Blaze

47

grinned, unless he'd had a girl as pretty as Señorita Carla gazing at him with frightened eyes.

He dug his heels into his mount to catch up with the man he was beholden to — twice.

★ ★ ★

Amos Brewster heard the sounds he'd been dreading, those of horses' hoofs and the jangling of saddle irons: the Slash Y had arrived. He looked out of the store window and counted six ranch hands with Lafe Simpson, the man who lived in the big house, at their head. Amos cast his daughter, who had joined him, a worried, angry glance.

'You should have taken heed of me, girl!' he snapped. 'Gone to stay with your Aunt Sofia where you'd be out of harm's way.'

'Why should there be any trouble here, Pa?' Carla asked. 'You didn't shoot those ranch hands.'

'That I didn't,' replied Amos. 'But

48

those hands were gunned down by men we were accommodating and old man Simpson will want to know all we can tell him about the pair.' He gave a wry grin. 'Which, thankfully, isn't much. Though he isn't the man who's got me worried, Carla, it's his roughneck crew that's the problem. They'll not take kindly hearing that two of their bunkhouse buddies have been shot. They've ridden here to do some shooting of their own. Especially Pete Drummond, he's with them. He'll want someone to pay for the killing of his brother and won't be fussy who it is if he can't get the men who did it.'

Carla's face drained of blood; her father's fears were getting to her. Both of the Drummonds had tried to force their attentions on her. She was thinking that it would have been wiser to have gone and stayed with her Aunt Sofia, but she couldn't have left her father to face the trouble he was expecting on his own. She wanted to stand resolutely alongside him as though she was the son her father had always wanted.

With his pistol fisted Pete Drummond burst into the store. His mad-eyed glare swept around the room seeking out the men who had shot Bull. Then his eyes focused on Carla. And Carla's true grit stance crumpled.

'Where are the sonsuvbitches?' he yelled.

'The pair rode out after the shooting, Pete,' replied a nerve-jangling Brewster. 'They were just a coupla drifters. I haven't seen them in San Remo before!'

Giving out a roar like an arrow-shot buffalo, Pete swung down his pistol and cracked open the sutler's head, felling him to the floor. Mad with rage at not being able to avenge his brother's death he began to kick Brewster's inert body.

A screaming bobcat of a Carla flung herself at Pete, clawing at his face. Pete cursed with pain and grabbed her. Feeling the warm softness of her body set his blood racing. He held the wildly struggling Carla with his gun hand and with the other he tore open her blouse, baring her breasts. Lewdly grinning, Pete reached down. Carla kicked out wildly in a last attempt to break out of her attacker's grip.

'Leave the girl be, Drummond!' Simpson barked from the doorway. 'Molesting her won't help us to find the men who gunned down your brother.' He glared at Pete. 'M'be the sutler could have told us what they looked like if you hadn't cold-cocked him.'

Simpson was a hard, unbending man who had carved a big cattle spread out of a land just as uncompromising. He would lose no sleep if he'd had to hang a twelve-year-old Mexican boy for stealing a maverick, but he drew the line at the raping of a young girl. There were many Mexicans farming close to his land and he wanted to be the gringo don in their eyes, not the cursed Yankee who allowed his men to ravish young Mexican girls. A reluctant Pete let go of Carla who, ignoring her nakedness, dropped to the floor to tend to her father.

'Give her a hand to get him out into the street, Pete,' Simpson said. 'When he comes to I can question him about his two sharp-shooting customers. While we're waiting, put a torch to this place — then it can't harbour any more killers of hard-working ranch hands.'

4

Boulder Rock, the first town they rode into since clearing the New Mexican border, raised Larribee's spirits somewhat. As well as having stores and other businesses, including two saloons and a bawdy house, running along each side of a broad Main Street, it was prosperous enough to have a stone-built bank. It wasn't as big as some of the banks he had heisted, but its strongroom should hold enough cash for him to pay his way a long time ahead.

Larribee could hear the snuffling and snorting of longhorns at the rear of Main Street, a herd, he thought, waiting to be driven to the nearest rail town. It would be a cattlemen's bank. Larribee smiled. He could be opening the gates to a small eldorado.

A sodbusters' bank held very little hard cash. Its safe would be stuffed with the promissory notes of the dirt farmers one payment ahead of foreclosure. Ranchers were a tight-fisted breed of men, paying their hands wages an Indian wouldn't work for, banking their spare cash to buy more cows so that they could become cattle kings like Charlie Goodnight and John Chisum.

Larribee gave the bank a close-eyed, assaying look as they headed for the livery barn and could spot no private guards standing on its stoop — another point in his favour if he did take the chance and rob the bank.

Blaze knew what was passing through Larribee's mind by the old man's changing expressions. He was eye-balling the bank with the intensity of a horse dealer checking out the fine lines of a pure blood stallion.

Tongue in cheek he said, 'Are you figurin' on takin' up your old trade, Mr Larribee?'

Larribee twisted in his saddle in surprise, then broke into a grin. 'It's early days yet, boy, early days,' he said.

'Things need workin' out. A half thought-out raid could get me shot. I need to scout around the territory a piece, find out the fastest way to the Mex border before I point my pistol at the bank tellers. I can't asskick it back to New Mexico and head into the trouble we're ridin' away from and, as you can see, the Western Union sonsuvbitches are here.'

Blaze noticed the line of posts lining Main Street, then, like some branchless trees, stretched out across the open plain as far as he could see.

'Yeah, I can see,' he replied. 'Within a coupla minutes of you running outa the bank most of Arizona will know that the Boulder Rock bank has been robbed and what the fella looks like.' He paused for a few seconds before saying, 'I've never robbed a bank before, Mr Larribee; me and the Boys lifted cattle and horses, but I'm willin' to act as your back-up.'

Larribee cast him a jaundiced-eyed look. 'I'm a loner, allus was, allus will be. No offence, boy, but fellas have a regular habit of dyin' the hard way when you're close by.'

He cut off Blaze's angry protest with a raised hand. 'I know, I know it ain't your doin' the killin's back there in New Mexico, but that don't alter the fact that you're a jinx. Killin' trouble kinda comes sneakin' up on you. You're ridin' with what the Injuns call the Death Shadow.'

Death Shadow my ass, Blaze thought angrily, piqued at Larribee's opinion of him as they drew up outside the livery barn. He'd just been unlucky meeting up with trouble being in the wrong place at the wrong time, or so he tried to convince himself.

Though he admitted, albeit reluctantly, that when he had ridden with Billy and the rest of the Boys, hell-raising and lifting John Chisum's cattle and the shooting and killings they indulged in, a whole posse of Death Shadows must have ridden with them.

For some unexplained reason, as he

swung down from his saddle, Blaze cast a nervous glance over his shoulder half expecting to see the Death Shadow mounted up on a big, black, fire-breathing horse. Jesus, he thought, the old bastard's ramblings would have him too scared to be in night camp on his own out there on the lonely plains if he didn't get a grip of himself.

'We'd better split up, boy,' Larribee said now, standing alongside him. 'If we're bein' trailed, the sonsuvbitches will be lookin' for a man and a boy. It don't make sense to make it easier for them to find us.' He handed Blaze a few crumpled dollar bills. 'I don't reckon you're carryin' any spendin' money,' he said gruffly, 'so that oughta find you a bed and grain for your horse for a few days until you decide what you intend doin'. I'm bookin' a bed in that roomin'-house we passed comin' in. You do likewise in that lodgin' house across the street there.' He favoured Blaze with a hard-eyed look. 'And for Pete's sake, try and keep outa trouble,

OK? If I'm goin' to rob this bank I want the town to be as quiet and peaceful as it is right now.'

Blaze took the offered money with a just as gruff, 'Thank you'. He was definitely going to steer clear of trouble even if that meant walking around the town minus his gunbelt. If the old fart did rob the bank he would maybe need help to make his getaway. He wanted to be around to make sure that the man he was beholden to came to no harm.

After coming out of the livery barn the pair exchanged brief handshakes, Blaze again thanking Larribee for saving his hide, then they went their own separate ways.

★　★　★

It had been two days since Larribee and Blaze had ridden into Boulder Rock, two well-spent days for Larribee, watching the routine activity of the bank staff and its customers, and checking out the fastest trail to the

Mexican border. His old bank-heisting confidence was returning. Taking the bank's cash, Larribee thought, would be as easy as robbing a candy store. Within an hour of coming out of the bank with the money bags, he'd be in old Mexico. With his haul of Yankee greenbacks he could live in the rich style of a don grandee owning a big *ranchero*, his bank-robbing days over for good. He was so sure he could successfully pull off the raid that he decided to pay a visit to the whore-house to kind of make up for the sudden ending of his pleasuring at Silver Sands.

Blaze was bellied up to the bar in the Golden Horseshoe, hanging on to his beer. He had called in the other saloon in town, The Wild Drover but there were only three drinkers in the place, sour-faced men, and Blaze was still young enough to crave lively company. The Golden Horseshoe with a couple of dozen drinkers or so and four saloon girls moving around the customers and laughing loudly at their good-natured joshing, suited his temperament.

Blaze couldn't afford to buy any of the girls a drink but after all the hair-raising trouble he had run into since riding south, then meeting up with the po-faced Mr Larribee, female laughter had him believing he was living once more.

He was close enough to the two drinkers at his end of the bar, cowhands he judged, to pick up the odd word of their conversation. He heard the sutler's store at San Remo mentioned by one of the men and his ears pricked up. Then his attention was distracted by one of the girls coming up to him and putting her arm around his waist asking him if he would buy her a drink.

Blaze turned and looked at the blonde girl with her skin-deep welcoming smile. He was close enough to feel her scented body heat through the thinness of her knee-length dress. His blood began to fire up and he was all set to spend some of his small poke on her by sleeping under the stars, that is until he heard the drinker closest to him say, 'Pete was sure enjoyin' himself pawing at that purty Mex 'breed girl back there in San Remo before the boss stopped him, Saul. And I was all set to join in the fun.'

'It ain't too late to try your hand, Cal,' replied Saul. 'We can swing by San Remo on the way back to the Slash Y. The girl, I reckon, will be stayin' with some greaser family bein' that her pa's store was burnt down. And he can't stop you handlin' his daughter, not after the beatin' up Pete dished out to him.'

The girl stepped back sharply from Blaze in sudden alarm at the dramatic change in his features. She thought she had been sparking up to a fresh-faced cowhand but the face she was smiling at had changed. It was the stone-eyed face of a border hard man, brutal men who occasionally rode into town. Men she wanted no dealings with even if they promised to buy her the fizzy

French wine the saloon sold by the bucketful.

Eyes glazed with a killing rage, Blaze left the girl and sidled up close to the man who wanted his way with Señorita Carla Brewster; close enough to nudge his elbow and cause him to spill the shot glass of whiskey he was holding.

A scowling Cal jerked round. 'You clumsy sonuvabitch!' he barked. 'You've made me spill my drink!'

Blaze beady-eyed Cal. 'Is molestin' young girls all assholes like you and that bastard, Pete, got the backbone for, *amigo*?'

Cal's scowl deepened into a red-eyed mask of rage. 'What the hell has it got to do with you, bub?' he snarled, and his hand dropped to his gun.

In a blur of movement Blaze grabbed hold of the whiskey bottle standing on the bar top and laid it hard against Cal's head, shattering the bottle and splitting Cal's head open in a bloody streak from temple to chin. Without so much as a groan Cal slumped sideways against Saul before folding at the knees and slipping to the floor to lie there in an untidy crumpled heap. Blaze's attack had been so swift and unexpected that it took Saul a few seconds to get over the shock of seeing Cal put down, then, cursing loudly, he grabbed for his gun.

Though Blaze wasn't carrying a gun he wasn't foolish enough to walk about a strange town without any means of defending himself, especially when he knew that back along his trail were men who wanted his blood. He leaned over Cal's body and jabbed the long bladed knife he'd had stuffed down his right boot, deep into Saul's gun arm.

Saul let out a howl of pain and dropped his gun. His cry drew everyone in the saloon's attention to the disturbance at the bar. There came a rattle of chairs being hastily pushed back and Blaze found himself ringed in by a mob of hostile-faced men who had seen a kid stranger viciously attack two regular drinkers for no reason at all. Blaze heard a growled, 'The bastard kid's loco! Let's get him, boys, before he does any more harm with that knife!' and he knew it was time he got to hell out of the Golden Horseshoe or he could be facing another hanging. His way out by the front door was blocked so, without wasting any more time, he vaulted over the bar counter and bolted for the rear door. A barkeep made a half-hearted attempt to stop him but a snarling Blaze brandished the knife in his face and he hastily drew back.

With yells of, 'Get out front some of you, and cut the bastard off!' ringing in his ears Blaze burst though the rear door of the saloon. Being in many a tight spot when riding with Bill Bonney, Blaze could think fast on the move. Dashing along the alley and on to Main Street was running into shooting trouble. Heading back along the alley and stumbling his way across the back lots in the dark would only put off his capture, or death, by a few minutes, though he had to make his pursuers think that they had failed to box him in.

He dropped to the ground and crawled his way under the eighteen-inch or so clearance beneath the saloon and its foundations hoping, briefly, that it wasn't the night haunt of one of the town's cur dogs, or a rattler's nest.

With his nerves screwed up tight he strengthened his grip on the knife. He would know in a second or two whether or not he had made a good move or he had got himself trapped like some cornered rat, a situation in which his knife would be useless as a defensive weapon. Blaze shivered. The Death Shadow was tapping *him* on the shoulder.

Then there came the pounding of boots on the rear door steps and he caught a faint glimpse of knee-high legs in front of him. Hardly daring to breathe he inched his way further into the deeper darkness beneath the saloon's floor.

'He ain't come this way!' he heard a distant voice shout. Then much closer came, 'He'll be cuttin' across the back lots! We've got the sonuvabitch by the balls, he'll never make it across Willow crick, it's in flood! Stretch out and form a picket line and move slowly, then we can hear him ploughing his way through the brush!' Again Blaze heard the sound of running feet and the whooping of men looking forward to a shooting.

He listened for a few anxious moments but couldn't hear or see any signs of movement in the alley and his sweat of fear began to cool. The silence gave Blaze time to reflect, angrily, on the situation he had landed himself in. If he'd controlled his temper he could have ridden back to San Remo and been of some help to Carla Brewster and her pa. His mad-assed action in attacking the two ranch hands had scotched that mercy mission. He'd be spotted for sure if he tried to go to his room for his gunbelt and the rest of his gear. Likewise if he made an attempt to pick up his horse bedded down in the livery barn.

Maybe, the wildly thinking Blaze thought, Mr Larribee would help him out, again. Though, realistically, he opined that the old man would probably shoot lumps off him. Mr Larribee had warned him not to raise any trouble in town so that he could go ahead with his plan to rob the bank. He had just raised up a big hunt, and he being the hunted, trouble couldn't come any thicker.

Whatever he decided Blaze knew that he couldn't stay holed-up under the saloon for any length of time. Come daylight and the swift rising of the sun some dog could come crawling in alongside him and, as he knew, cur dogs were not noted for their friendliness to humans, or each other. It would start barking, a racket that would bring out the saloon owner into the alley wondering what varmint was bedded down under his saloon. And the townsfolk would get themselves a lynching.

Blaze elbowed his way into the alley,

lying prone there for several moments until he was certain that all the shouting he was hearing was coming from the back lots. Then he sprang to his feet and ran to the end of the alley, his knife held ready for one last suicidal stand. He paused there for a quick but all-seeing look both ways along the street. It was deserted, every male in town must be floundering their way through the wild tangle of land at the rear of the street. Luck was swinging his way a little. Resisting the urge to dash across the street he walked tall and slow, like a man who had nothing more on his mind than a quiet evening stroll. Itchy-backed he stepped on to the porch of the rooming-house without any yells of, 'There's the bastard!' sounding behind him. Cat-footed he made his way to the outside stairs that led to the first floor and the rented rooms.

★ ★ ★

An inner smiling Larribee came down from one of the upstairs rooms. The girl had been worth her price and she'd put him in a relaxed, good-feeling mood and there and then he made the decision to rob the bank in the morning. This time tomorrow he would be addressed as Señor Larribee, a rich gringo generously buying drinks for every peon in the cantina, giving a knowing wink to the prettiest *señorita* in the place. His smile showed openly on his face as he walked into the cat-house lounge. He idly noticed that many of the girls were sitting about in the room. The place had been crowded with potential customers when he'd come in an hour ago.

'Ain't you goin' to join the hunt, mister?' a girl sitting near the door asked him.

'Hunt? What hunt is that?' a puzzled Larribee replied.

'Why the hunt for the loco kid who almost killed those two ranch hands in the Golden Horseshoe Saloon,' another girl butted in. 'He cracked a whiskey bottle over one of the hands' heads and stabbed his buddy in the arm. Every goddamned horn-dog in the town is out there tryin' to track him down. That kid's sure lost us a lot of business tonight.'

Larribee's smile sickened and died away, likewise his good-humoured feelings. His life of high living below the border wasn't about to start in the morning. The kid's wild streak had shown up again and this time he had stirred up a whole town. This time, he thought grimly, the crazy kid would have to fend for himself, which didn't put him out any. It wasn't as though they had been regular pards. In fact, he cursed himself for being so softhearted as to get himself involved in the kid's life.

Back in the rooming-house, Larribee unlocked the door to his room and heard a slight noise at the far end of the narrow passage. He turned sharply and by the flickering flame of the solitary wall lantern he saw Blaze stepping out of what he took to be a closet.

'Are you here to stab me with that pig sticker you're holdin', boy?' he growled.

'No I ain't, Mr Larribee,' Blaze replied indignantly. 'Why would I do that?'

'By what I've heard,' Larribee said, 'you've been kinda free and easy with that knife, and a whiskey bottle.'

'It weren't like that at all!' Blaze said his anger rising.

Larribee gave out with a snorting laugh. 'Did you kinda accidentally bump into those two fellas holdin' the knife and the bottle? That's not the way those fellas who're huntin' for you see it!'

'I'd appreciate it if you'd let me come into your room and hear me out,' pleaded Blaze. 'It'll only take a coupla minutes. I don't want you to think that I put down those two sonsuvbitches just because I got the urge to see blood flow.'

Larribee eyed Blaze for a few weighing-up seconds before heeling his door open and saying, 'You've got those two minutes then you vamoose, *comprende*?'

Larribee wanted to get into his room to be within snatching distance of his gun hanging on the bed end. He did some silent cursing. Going into the cat house unarmed wanting to look like a civilized gent was a false pride that could get him killed. He indicated that Blaze should sit on the only chair in the room while he dropped down on to the bed, only inches away from his gunbelt. He didn't know Blaze at all. He had heard enough talk about Billy the Kid's Boys to know that they were an unstable bunch of characters. One moment all smiles, the next blazing away with their big Colt .45 cannons. He kept a wary eye on Blaze. If the kid made a move against him a lot of folk in Boulder Rock were going to be disappointed, for he would blow the kid apart and prove his belief that the Boys were destined to die young.

'OK,' he said curtly. 'Say your piece, then git!'

In a few terse sentences Blaze told Larribee of hearing that the Slash Y crew had burned down Brewster's store, beat him up and molested Carla Brewster. Larribee's face grew tighter and meaner-looking as he listened to Blaze.

'Hearing the two sonsuvbitches laughing about how they were going to have their way with Señorita Carla when they rode back to San Remo kinda got my blood going,' Blaze said. 'So I did what I felt I oughta do.'

Blaze stopped speaking for a few moments giving time for Larribee to think that he would have gone for the pair the way the kid had.

Blaze started up again. 'I'll admit I made the wrong move, Mr Larribee,' he said. 'It's prevented me from getting hold of my horse and gear and riding back to San Remo to watch over Mr Brewster and his daughter.' He looked

Larribee directly in the eye. 'All I'm asking for is a pistol and a handful of shells. I can easily lift a saddled horse, then I'll be on my way.' Face twisting in anger, he added, 'Then by hell I'll gut-shoot any Slash Y ranch hand who tries to lay his dirty paws on the girl!'

Larribee's blood ran cold as he held Blaze's wild-eyed glare. Jesus, he thought, it was a wonder the kid had lived so long. The young hellion showed no sign of fear at the odds he was taking on. But it was his as well as the kid's doing that had brought trouble on the Brewster family, so it was beholden on him to do no less than the kid, to make sure that they would get no more grief from the Slash Y,

'So what's it to be, Mr Larribee?' he heard Blaze say. 'Are you gonna oblige me or not?'

'You know what we'll be facin', kid,' he said. 'A ranch crew of hard *hombres*.'

'We?' said a surprised Blaze.

'We're both to blame for what has

74

happened to the Brewsters,' Larribee said 'and it's up to the two of us to put things right for them. Though it ain't goin' to be easy takin' on fourteen m'be eighteen men. We can't just go fireballin' in on the Slash Y and gun them all down in a face-to-face shoot-out like you and Billy would favour. We'll need to think up some sort of a plan so we can get the edge on the sonsuvbitches.' He gimlet-eyed Blaze. 'So I'd be obliged if you didn't go off at half-cock again.'

Bending down he picked up his saddle-bags. Unbuckling one of the pouches he took out a pistol and a box of shells and handed them to Blaze. 'Load it up then stuff it down the top of your pants; keep the rest of the reloads. I'll go and knock up the livery-barn owner and pick up my horse.' He cold-grinned. 'If I show him my fierce bank robber's face it could persuade the old goat to give me your mount as well. You stay here till you see me pass by rein-leadin' your horse, then sneak out but don't attempt to get into your saddle till we're well clear of this hornets' nest, OK? Some of the fellas huntin' you could come driftin' back on to the street.'

'OK,' replied Blaze, then began thumbing loads into the chamber of the Colt, hoping that Mr Larribee would soon come up with a plan that would enable him to send the shells he was handling winging into the dirty hides of the Slash Y crew.

With his pistol belted around his waist Larribee slung his saddle-bag over his shoulder, then picking up his rifle he left Blaze to it, but not before giving him a final warning glare then closing the door behind him.

★　★　★

A lip-chewing, impatient Blaze waited at the window for the sighting of Mr Larribee up on his horse towing his along as well. It had seemed a long time since the old man had left but he'd heard no sounds of gunfire coming from the direction of the livery barn so he guessed that everything was going fine for Mr Larribee. Patience was a trait that the Boys didn't have. They lived fast, rode fast, shot fast, and some of them had died fast. Though hair-triggered as he was, Mr Larribee's orders for him to stay low made lifesaving sense. Already men who had quit tracking him were coming out of the alleys. Apart from putting himself in danger if he acted foolishly he would be putting Mr Larribee's life at risk, a man he was beholden to.

Larribee slowly rode his horse along Main Street trailing Blaze's mount behind him, thinking that robbing banks was easier on his nerves. Even in the weak light from the few lanterns dotted along the street he couldn't be mistaken for the kid but it would only need one man to recollect seeing him riding into town with Blaze and understand the reason for the spare horse, then it would be thinking of number one as the lead began to fly, leaving Blaze to get out of Boulder Rock the best way he could.

He had had no trouble getting hold of the horses; the livery barn doors were wide open and he'd found the owner stretched out in one of the stalls with an empty whiskey bottle lying beside him. Larribee grinned at the situation. In different circumstances he and Blaze could have made off with every horse in the stable. He saddled up his and Blaze's horse with some haste, slipping a couple of dollar bills between the fingers of the sleeping owner before he left. Larribee still had his pride: he only robbed banks. Now here he was, riding into a shooting hell if things went bad on him. He glanced to his right as he passed the rooming-house but saw no signs of Blaze — the kid had taken his warning to heart.

He had cleared Main Street and was now riding across the open range and still Blaze hadn't shown up. He was beginning to wonder if he'd met up with trouble coming out of the rooming-house when he heard a slight scuffling noise behind him and jerked his head round. A wide-grinning Blaze was sitting up on his horse.

'Any trouble back there, Mr Larribee?' asked Blaze.

'No trouble at all,' replied Larribee. 'As you can see I managed to borrow a long gun for you. Now let's get clear of this burg, boy; we've got enough trouble ahead of us without it snappin' at our asses,' and he dug his heels into his horse's ribs.

Blaze didn't worry about possible trouble; if it came then was the time to fret. He was thinking that he would be seeing Señorita Carla Brewster again. His face hardened as he urged his mount into a gallop.

5

They crossed the New Mexico line at a ground-eating pace, riding in silence, each deep in his own thoughts. Larribee was worrying about how he could carry out the promise he'd given to Blaze, that of how the trouble they had unintentionally sicced on to the store-keeper and his daughter would be settled in their favour.

Blaze had no such brain-racking thoughts. His plan of action was quite simple: to gun down any Slash Y man who so much as cast a lewd glance at Señorita Brewster. Then, when the chance came, burn down the Slash Y's big house to even things up somewhat for Mr Brewster.

Larribee had another problem chewing away at him — his pard Blaze. While the kid had the knack of getting himself into trouble he'd also proved that he was capable of hauling himself out of it, leaving dead and beat-up men behind him. But the fight they were about to start against the big odds of the Slash Y would have to be fought hit and run guerilla style and he didn't think Blaze had the patience to hold back his wild, charging-in temperament. Larribee reckoned it was time he got nosy about what made the boy who was going to walk the line with him tick. His, 'Why did you quit ridin' with the Boys?' cut off Blaze's pleasant thoughts of seeing Carla once more.

'Eh, what?' Blaze said.

'I asked why you left William Bonney,' Larribee said. 'If it don't upset you any tellin' me.'

'I ain't offended, Mr Larribee,' replied Blaze. 'I just didn't agree with Billy's change of mind. And that kinda upset me.'

'How come?' a puzzled Larribee asked.

'You've got to know the situation up there in Lincoln County, Mr Larribee,'

Blaze said. 'There's a —'

'I know all about the shootin' war goin' on there between Murphy and Chisum, Blaze,' interrupted Larribee. He narrowed-eyed Blaze. 'I also heard tell that William Bonney was lined up with the Murphy faction.'

'Not any more, Mr Larribee,' replied Blaze. 'He's hired his guns to John Chisum. Me and the boys had a good thing going riding for Murphy. He paid us well to lift Chisum's cows, burn down his line cabins, and hold up the Jingle Bob's supply wagons. Mr Murphy had a hankerin' to be the big man in the county, not John Chisum. Then for a reason I ain't figured out, Billy took Chisum's gold. I told him that it was a low-down trick and that we should honour our deal with Murphy who, I told you, treated us real well.'

Blaze thin-smiled. 'But you don't tell Billy what he oughta do if you want to keep walking around. Now you may have me tagged as a hair-triggered *pistolero*, Mr Larribee but I ain't so

82

loco as to take on Chisum's hard men and Billy and my old *compadres*, so, like you, I came south.'

'Yeah, just like me,' Larribee muttered. 'Exchanging gettin' shot in the north of the territory to riskin' gettin' plugged in this stretch of real estate.'

'That's m'be so, Mr Larribee,' Blaze said. 'But I ain't frettin'. It's the first time I'm using my gun without bein' paid to do so and it's giving me a good feeling not havin' to shoot some poor fella on the say-so of a high and mighty boss man.'

Larribee began to reassess his opinion of Blaze. Loyalty was a trait he'd never expected from a hired gun. Being a loner he'd never had cause to be loyal to anyone but himself and Logan. He'd no doubts now that the kid, if he kept a tight rein on him, would be as good a man as any to ride the line with. Then he heard Blaze ask if he'd come up with a plan.

'No, I ain't, boy,' he said. 'Except that we're gonna need help if we're goin' to get the better of the Slash Y boys. Or get real lucky.'

Blaze pondered on how they could hire a gang of hard-riding men when they had no more than a few dollars between them. Though he didn't mention his confused thinking to his partner.

* * *

Nearing the huddle of buildings that was San Remo Larribee and Blaze drew back their mounts, finally pulling them to a halt when they had clear sighting of the charred, broken ruins of the sutler's stores. Larribee heard Blaze muttering and wondered how so young a boy had come by so many curse words, words that would have shamed a mule skinner.

He swung sharply around in his saddle to face Blaze. 'Curb your language, boy,' he snapped. 'Or you'll be spoutin' such-like words in front of that purty young girl you fancy seein' again!'

Blaze knew that Larribee had made a fair point. He didn't want the *señorita* to think badly of him. Though he did wonder if the old goat ever showed openly how he was feeling. 'Where do you think Miss Carla and her pa are, Mr Larribee?' he asked.

Larribee gave Blaze a flint-eyed look. 'Once we start hittin' the Slash Y the boss man will kick over every stone in the territory to find us,' he said. 'Question every *gringo*, Mex, Injun hereabouts, if they've spotted any men ridin' across this land they ain't seen before. And that askin' will include the Brewsters.' Larribee's face softened slightly. 'Now I've a hankerin' to partake of that fine chow that young girl put before us again Blaze, but we don't want to bring another heap of trouble to their door so we stay well clear of them. Then the Brewsters can speak the truth if approached by the Slash Y crew that they don't know who it is that's causin' all the trouble for Simpson. And they ain't seen us since we pulled outa San Remo.'

85

Larribee took another long look at the burnt-out store before he came out with a curt, 'OK, boy, let's do some scoutin' before we start raisin' hell. I reckon that the regular trips of the Slash Y supply wagon to San Remo must have cut a trail to the ranch's home range even a coupla white-eyes could follow.' He dug his heels into Logan's flanks and, as the horse moved forward, he called over his shoulder, 'Be ready to go to ground pronto if we see the dust of any riders.'

It was a greatly disappointed Blaze who urged his horse into a trot. He had hoped to have the pleasure of talking to the young *señorita* again but once more his old partner had spoken sense. While the fight they were about to start wasn't as big as the one he'd taken part in up there in Lincoln County, like all wars, big or small, innocent folk could get hurt. The Brewsters had already paid a painful price; he didn't want to be responsible for putting them in harm's way for the second time.

6

It was Jack, handing out mugs of coffee to the branding crew, who first saw Saul and Cal riding in. 'The boys are back from Boulder Rock, boss!' he called out. Then added a gasped, 'By heck they're both bandaged up!'

Lafe Simpson, overseeing the tallying of the mavericks that were being branded, put down his coffee on the tailgate of the chuck wagon and took in Saul's strapped-up right arm and Cal's bandaged head. His face stiffened in anger. He knew he bossed over a wild crew and that he had to allow them to blow off steam occasionally, but the two sons-of-bitches seemed to have taken part in one hell of a fight, and come off worse.

'I expected you boys back here a coupla hours ago!' he snapped. 'I don't pay you to get into fights!'

'We didn't get into a fight, boss!' Saul said protestingly, wincing as he slowly dismounted, his arm useless. He cast a painful look up at Cal. 'Ain't that the truth, *amigo*?'

Cal, whose lacerated face was burning with a fiery pain, managed a croaking, 'It was as Saul said. We were just standin' at the bar in the Golden Horseshoe havin' a drink before we rode out when this loco kid came up to us and cracked a bottle over my head. It was only when I came to that I found out the sonuvabitch had knifed Saul in the arm. We had to pay a visit to the doc's to get our wounds seen to, boss, that's why we're late.'

Simpson gave them both a suspicious-eyed glare. More than likely, he thought, the horn dogs had got into a fight over the favours of a two-dollar whore. By the state they were in he reckoned it would be a while before they started brawling again but the sons-of-bitches still had to earn their due.

'Get back to the ranch,' he said. 'See

to your horses and get some rest before the pair of you take over the night riding of the south herd.'

It was another awkward, painful chore for Saul to get back into his saddle. Before they could swing their horses' heads round Jack said, 'That kid who knifed you, Saul, was he on his own? Or did he have an older, horse-faced-lookin' man taggin' along with him?'

'Naw, the bastard was on his own,' Saul replied. 'A drifter, I figure, as he hadn't been seen in Boulder Rock before.'

'Why the question about the kid, Jack?' a quizzical-eyed Simpson asked.

Jack shrugged. 'It might mean damn all, boss, but remember it was a young kid who gunned down Bull. Though he had a pard with him, an older man, the fella who crippled poor Caleb. They were strangers in the territory. It could be they headed for Boulder Rock when they rode out of San Remo.'

'You're thinking that the same kid

who did for Bull knifed Saul and cracked open Cal's head?' Simpson said.

Jack shrugged again. 'Could be, boss, though I'll admit that Arizona must have a whole heap of home-raised kid shootists.'

Lafe Simpson did some fast recollecting. Jack's reasoning was not so way out. He'd built up the Slash Y the hard way, stomping on men who had stood in his way. There'd be a whole string of men lined up wanting to take him down. Though a young kid and an old man ought not to cause him much uneasiness even if they had cost him a straw boss and a top hand and another two of his crew roughed up. Unless, he thought worriedly, they were part of a gang. Then his face took on the hard-eyed look of the taking man he was.

'You boys get back to the ranch,' he grated. He waited until the pair were on their way, then he swung round to eyeball Jack. 'You grab hold of Phil's horse, Jack, and ride to San Remo and see if those two *pistoleros* have shown up there again; you know what they look like. Make enquires about them in the cantina and of any Mex who isn't having his *siesta*.'

'But what about the chuck wagon, boss?' Jack said, with a touch of desperation in his voice. 'All my cookin' gear needs washin' and stowin' away.'

Jack wasn't overjoyed about making the trip to San Remo on his ownsome. It was all right Simpson telling him that he knew the kid and his pard, but that meant they knew him, knew him as a Slash Y man. If they were picking a fight with the Slash Y then he was dead meat. He was no *pistolero*, he was a cook. He wondered why they hadn't shot him down alongside Bull and Caleb but he opined that with a young girl being present they had curbed their shooting spree.

'We'll see to the wagon,' Simpson said, with some heat to the miserable-faced Jack. He waved a dismissive hand.

'Now get up on Phil's horse, pronto, and start raising the dust on the San Remo trail.'

Dirty-mouthing under his breath, Jack walked across to the horse line.

Simpson glared angrily at the branding crew. 'Now let's get finished here before nightfall!' He didn't tell them that he was going to double the night guard on both herds and the ranch buildings. With the possibility that hard men were picking a fight with him, and had already made their mark, he couldn't risk not being extra vigilant.

★　★　★

'Cabin up ahead on the far side of the wagon trail, Mr Larribee!' the keener-sighted Blaze called out. 'You can just see the smoke pipe stickin' above that ridge!'

Larribee swivelled his gaze round to his left and being taller in the saddle saw the weathered planking of the cabin's sloping roof, and the thin wind-blown wisps of smoke coming out of the chimney. His face steeled over.

'Swing down, boy,' he said. 'That cabin's occupied. Head for that stand of timber! We'll take a closer look on foot.'

As they dismounted, Larribee gave Blaze a twist of a smile. 'I know, you bein' a young hellraiser, you're thinkin' than I'm actin' like a skittery old maid, but the only edge we've got is to keep Simpson off-balance, like wonderin' and worryin' about the number of men he's facin'. If he knows there are only two of us he'll have every man on his payroll seekin' us out. Even the cook and his cat.'

Rein-leading their horses into the screen of the trees Blaze thought that Billy Bonney and the Boys had a lot to learn on how to fight a small war if they wanted to be still moving around after the shooting had ended. He'd more chance of staying alive the old brush boy way Mr Larribee intended fighting.

Larribee had also got serious thoughts on his mind. They were now on Slash Y range, the battleground, and the boy would be expecting him to state his plan of action, or he'd think of him as a blow hard. Right now all he could come up with to begin their fight against the Slash Y was to burn down one ramshackle line cabin and make sure that the man, or men, inside weren't fit to tend Simpson's cows for a long spell by winging them.

They tied up the horses and, drawing out their long guns from their saddle boots, crossed the wagon trail, dropping to the ground near the crest, to belly crawl the rest of the way.

From that vantage point they had a clear view of the cabin, the three horses tethered out front and the hanging about to take place on the far side of the shallow creek. Under the only tree on the plain two widely grinning Slash Y were holding a frantically struggling Mexican youth. The third ranch hand, also seeing the humour in the situation, was throwing a hanging rope across the stoutest branch of the tree.

Blaze brought his rifle up to his shoulder and for the second time since they had ridden together Larribee heard him dirty-mouthing. Before Blaze could squeeze the trigger Larribee laid a restraining hand on his shoulder.

'We're only goin' to wing the sonsuvbitches, *comprende*, boy?' he said hard-voiced. 'We don't want to be branded as no-good killers.'

Blaze gave him a savage-faced glare then concentrated in drawing a bead on his target and for a split-second Larribee thought that Blaze was past taking orders from him. Blaze's rifle cracked and flamed and it was with great relief Larribee heard the screeching howl of pain from the rope wielding man who dropped to the ground clutching at his shattered right knee. 'I figure that's knocked the smile off your face, mister,' he heard Blaze say.

The other two Slash Y men let go of the Mexican boy and made a dash for the shelter of the thick trunk of the would-be hanging tree. Blaze cut loose another cruel crippling leg shot, tumbling one of the running men to the ground in mid-stride, to lie there thrashing in agony.

'That'll do for starters, boy, I think they've got the message that they ain't havin' a hangin' today,' Larribee said, thinking that he wouldn't like to face Blaze with a gun when the kid's blood was running wild. He was a natural born shootist, and not at cans on a split rail fence.

Blaze yelled something in Mexican, Larribee only making out, 'Vamoose, pronto!' He saw that the boy didn't vamoose but just stood there under the tree looking apprehensively over his shoulder. Larribee thought it was time he played his part. Bringing up his rifle he fired a rapid fusillade of shots at the base of the tree, then yelled, 'You, pilgrim, behind that tree, if you pull a gun on that Mex kid me and my boys will come down there and you'll have your lynchin'. Though you'll be wearing the hemp collar! Play it right and we'll leave you to see to your buddies!'

Butler, the ranch hand eating dirt behind the tree, was covered with ripped off shards of wood the shells had torn off the trunk. He wondered who the ambushers were. He opined that they must be a mixed band of Mexicans and Yankees; why else would they want to stop a greaser cattle rustler from being justly strung up? He also came to the quick conclusion that the son-of-a-bitch who had shouted out he would hang him, wasn't making an idle threat. Smithy and Tad had been shot down like cur dogs. And their moans and groans weren't making him any happier. He owed loyalty to Simpson but it didn't stretch to having a gunfight with a bunch of wild, killing men. He raised his head high enough from the ground to call out, 'The Mex kid can go where the hell he likes, mister, he'll get no trouble from me!' To add sincerity to his statement he drew out his pistol and threw it well clear of the tree.

'A wise decision, friend!' Larribee

shouted back. 'Now step out so we can see that you ain't about to go back on your word. And you, kid, get up on to this ridge, pronto!'

A churning-bowelled Butler shuffled crabways into the open, hands held high. Hoping to hell that the sharp-shooting son-of-a-bitch up on the ridge wasn't conning him, that he had every intention of gunning him down once he'd stepped in the clear. His face twisted into a tortuous looking mask anticipating the fearful agony of a Winchester shell tearing through his leg.

A wary-eyed Felix watched the *gringo* come into the open. Though he'd had two calls for him to make a run for it, one in Mexican, the other by a *gringo*, he couldn't move his legs; they felt as though they didn't belong to him. He was still in shock. Not five minutes ago he was almost pissing his pants, seconds from a fearful death, only consoled by the thought that Fierro and Gomez, his younger brothers, with him on the raid to steal one of the Slash Y cows, were still running free. Now this miracle had happened and he was free. Though Felix thought that miracles were performed by saints not by what seemed to be a band of *bandidos*.

'What the hell!' Larribee blurted out, as two Mexican boys suddenly appeared on the ridge to the left of him and Blaze, yelling their heads off. 'Where for Chris' sake did those two spring from, Blaze?'

Shouts of, 'Run, Felix, run!' from Fierro and Gomez standing in clear view on the high ground gave Felix back control of his frozen legs. He burst into a long loping run, the water splashing shoulder high as he crossed the creek then scrambled up the slope to the rimline, there to be embraced by his wide-smiling brothers.

'Find out who the kids are and the reason for the lynchin', Blaze,' Larribee said. 'And tell them to get off the skyline! If another Slash Y man comes ridin' in he'll pick them off with his rifle! I'll keep an eye on that fella down there just in case he has a change of mind and wants to make a fight of it.' Raising his voice he called, 'You can come across the crick and get the horses so you can take your buddies back to the ranch to get their wounds seen to. But unship the three rifles and lay them on the ground. Then you won't have the temptation to swing back and bushwhack us.'

* * *

Butler rope-led the horses, laden with the two wounded men laid over their saddles, back across the creek. He glared up at the ridge and yelled, 'Whoever you sonsuvbitches are, you're dead! The boss will hunt all of you down even if you're holed-up below the border!'

Larribee gave a thin-lipped grin as he listened to the ranch-hand's tirade. His makeshift plan was beginning to work. While Simpson and his crew were chasing their own asses trying to pick up the tracks of a bunch of riders, he and the kid could sneak by them and give Simpson another jab in the eye. He got to his feet when he lost sight of the trail dust of the three horses and walked down the ridge to where Blaze was chatting to the Mexican boys.

'This is Felix, Mr Larribee,' Blaze said, nodding to the boy who had escaped a lynching. 'And his two brothers, Gomez, the smaller one, and Fierro.'

'*Mucho gracias*, Señor Larribee, for saving my life,' Felix said. He reached out and gripped Larribee's hand in a firm handshake. He grinned as both his brothers spoke together in Mexican. 'They're also thanking you, *señor* for coming to the aid of what those ranch hands called a 'ragged-assed greaser kid'.' Then serious-faced, he added, 'And make enemies of the *mal hombres* who ride for the *gringo* dog, Simpson.'

'We've already made enemies of the Slash Y, boy,' replied Larribee, 'and I've never had a likin' to see any man or boy strung up.' He close-eyed Felix. 'I take it that you were caught tryin' to steal one of Simpson's cows.'

Felix didn't answer him; instead, he cast a searching gaze along the ridge. A puzzled expression crept over his face. 'Where are the rest of your *compadres*, Señor Larribee?' he asked. 'To aid you in your fight against the *gringo* rancher?'

'There ain't any *compadres*, boy,' Larribee replied. 'There's just me and Señor Blaze there.'

Felix's jaw dropped open. He gave Larribee then Blaze a wide-eyed disbelieving look. He'd been led to believe that most *gringos* were loco, none more so than the tall hard-faced *gringo* who had saved his life.

'I know what you're thinking, Felix,' Blaze grinned. 'M'be me and Señor Larribee are crazy but it's beholden on us to raise hell with Simpson and his crew. And the tally so far is in our favour. Three of Simpson's boys won't be sitting up in their saddles for quite a spell and one hand is now herdin' the Devil's cows down there in Hell.' No longer smiling, he added, 'If you and your brothers are stealin' Slash Y cows then you're liable to be standin' under a hangin' tree again.'

'We are not stealing, Señor Blaze!' Felix said angrily. 'We're taking from Simpson much less than he took from us!' His anger flared wildly in his eyes. 'And one day, if the Holy *Madre* smiles on us, we will kill that *gringo* dog!'

Then he told Blaze and Larribee that his father had once owned a herd of sheep, large enough to support his family. And how one morning Simpson and some of his crew rode up to their cabin and accused his father of allowing his sheep to pollute the creek water his cows drank from.

'My father told Simpson,' continued Felix. 'That the creek was not Yankee water, that it flowed north from Mexico but he was willing to share it with *gringo* cattle.'

103

Blaze wondered if Felix had Indian blood in him. His face was as savage-looking as a full-blood Comanche.

'Then Simpson shot dead my father,' Felix said, voice as hard and unyielding as his features. 'Then he had his men kill all our sheep. Before they rode out they burnt down our home, with our mother lying ill in bed inside. We are now living with my grandfather in a hut in the mountains. Like the wolves we have become. We steal Simpson's cattle to stay alive so we can carry out our sworn oath, to kill Simpson.'

Felix bold-eyed Larribee. 'M'be, Señor Larribee, we can fight Simpson together.'

The blunt directiness of Felix's proposal mentally rocked Larribee back on his heels. He was seeking allies in his fight against the Slash Y, grown men who could handle guns, not three ragged-assed Mexican kids. However much they hated Simpson, hate alone wouldn't bring the boys their just revenge on the killers of their folk. Only more guns could do that.

'Yeah, well, er,' he managed to stammer out. 'That's a real manly offer, Felix. But I reckon we ought to let your grandpa have his say in the matter, OK? This ain't the place or the time to discuss how we're goin' to make our moves against Simpson. You and your brothers go down and get yourselves a rifle apiece, then look inside the cabin and see if there's anything in there worth takin', coffee, cans of beans, whatever. Me and Blaze will search for a place where we can lead the horses down.' He grinned. 'Before we leave, you and your brothers can burn down that shack.' His look took in the three brothers. 'Off you go, *amigos*, the day ain't finished yet. I want you to take us to the herd from where you hoped to lift a cow so we can scatter it to hell and beyond — which oughta delay Simpson's hunt for us for a few days.'

Larribee and Blaze took hold of their horses' reins and walked them along the ridge. It was Blaze who spotted a likely way down to the flat, a faint game track that snaked its way down the slope. He pointed it out to his partner.

'If we hold on to their tails and dig our heels in, Mr Larribee,' he said, 'we oughta make it down to the crick without breakin' ours and the horses' legs.' He grinned as he watched the brothers aiming their rifles at mock targets. 'Are you goin' to take up Felix's offer, Mr Larribee? We're operatin' blind out here; those boys will know the lay of the land, know where the line cabins and the herds are bedded down.'

Larribee favoured Blaze with a dour-faced look. 'They're only kids!' he snapped. 'Do you want to see them dead?'

Blaze stood his ground. 'I ain't much older than Felix!' he snapped back. 'And as far as wantin' to see them dead, Felix is seeing to that on his own. We saved his neck bein' stretched. And they've sure got a stronger reason to take on Simpson than we have!'

Larribee thinking that he was having

to make more worrying decisions than he ever did in his bank-heisting days, gave a growled, 'I'll think about it. Now let's get our asses off this damn ridge before we get them shot off!'

★ ★ ★

Simpson, on the porch of the big house, was giving Pete Drummond, his new foreman, his orders for tomorrow's branding as Butler rode up bringing in the gunshot Smithy and Tod. 'Jesus Christ!' he gasped, after Butler had told him about the shooting at the cabin. Fear wasn't a weakness he possessed but his unknown attackers, and the 'why', were unnerving him somewhat. He cursed loudly. If he didn't put a goddamned stop to it he would soon be bossing over a crew of dead men and cripples. Then his frustrated anger took control.

'How the hell did a man and a boy jump the three of you?' he roared. 'I'm guessing that it was the same pair of bastards who gunned down Bull!'

'It weren't them, boss,' Butler replied with some heat. He was still shaking thinking how lucky he'd been not to have ended up painfully crippled like Smithy and Tod. 'It was a whole damn gang of them!'

'A gang!' Simpson repeated, frantically thinking that the trouble he was having so far could be only a mere skirmish in what could turn out to be a full blown range war. 'How many of the sonsuvbitches were there?' he asked.

'I don't rightly know,' Butler told him. 'The bastards were bellied down on the ridge above the line cabin. Me and the boys were just about to slip a rope collar round the neck of one of those greaser kids who are helpin' themselves to our cows, when a rifleman cut loose at us puttin' down Smithy and Tod with bad leg wounds. I got myself hunkered down behind the hangin' tree before they winged me. Then the sharp-shootin' bastard shouted out that if I didn't let the Mex kid go and show myself, unarmed, he would send his boys down to string me up!'

Noticing Simpson's doubting scowl Butler said defiantly, 'There was no way I could have fought them off, boss; they had me well and truly pinned down. And besides I had to think of poor Smithy and Tod lying there bleedin' and moanin' like stuck hogs so I told the kid to vamoose then tossed my pistol and rifle well clear of the tree and came out with my hands held high. They didn't cut loose at me but told me to get Smithy and Tod laid across their horses and to take them back to the ranch to get their wounds seen to.' Butler looked Simpson straight in the eyes and as more of an order than a suggestion, he said, 'Doc Bell oughta be brought out, pronto, to see that their wounds don't go bad on them.'

'Get them bedded down in the bunkhouse,' Simpson said, holding in his anger. He was four men short; he couldn't afford any man to quit on him thinking that he was riding roughshod over him. 'Then ride out to Placer Flats and get hold of the doc, OK?'

Simpson gazed unseeing past Butler as he headed the horses towards the bunkhouse. He ground his teeth in silent rage. He'd killed all colours and breeds of man to build up the Slash Y and he would gladly kill again to hold on to it. He came out of his trance, looked at Drummond and rapped out an order.

'Cancel the branding and bring all the men in. It's too late to set up a hunt for the bastards; they'll be holed-up in the hills someplace. But they aren't ghost riders, so no matter how carefully they move around, their horses will leave tracks. Send Jim Crow out at first light on a scout; if he's as good as he often says he is he'll know where to start to pick up their tracks. If he returns with good news we'll all ride out. Meanwhile the crew will stand guard here to protect the house and the barns until it is time to ride out for the kill.'

'Right, boss,' Drummond replied. 'I'll roust the night crew outa their bunks before I go.'

The sound of a hard-ridden horse had both men swinging round.

'What the hell's up with Cole!' Drummond blurted out. 'I ain't seen him rein-lash his horse since we got jumped by that Comanche warband the day we were roundin' up a bunch of strays close to the Mex border.'

Cole yanked his mount to a haunch-sliding halt in front of the porch.

'The Black Ridge herd's spooked, boss!' he cried. 'I left Clem and Lacey tryin' to turn 'em but the goddamned critters have got the bit between their teeth. I'll need the whole crew to bunch them up!'

Simpson stood stiff and expressionless-faced as though hewn from stone. There had been no lightning storms over the Black Ridge buttes so the herd hadn't been frightened and taken off — they had been deliberately stampeded. The sons-of-bitches, whoever they were, had hit him again. He smiled grimly. He had figured how the bastards were playing their hand. They intended running rings around him to provoke him to strike out blindly at them, leaving the ranch house and the barns undefended. Then they would close in for the kill. Only he was not playing the game the way they were forcing him to do. As much as he hated doing damn all, Simpson knew that it was the waiting time. Only if Jack came back from San Remo with clear intelligence of where the raiders were holed-up, or Jim Crow proved his worth tomorrow, he would keep his men here and let the bastards come to him.

He looked across at Cole, ass-shuffling in his saddle as he waited for his orders.

'Let the herd run, Cole,' he said. 'They'll bunch up when they get tired. Ride out and bring in Clem and Lacey.'

'Let the herd run, boss?' a surprised Cole repeated.

'You heard what Mr Simpson said,

Cole!' Pete Drummond growled. 'Get out there and bring in your crew, pronto like!'

Muttering oaths, Cole dragged his horse around, dug his heels savagely into its ribs, causing it to take off in the same dust-raising pace he had ridden in, thinking that the longhorns wouldn't run out of steam until they were trampling the dirt in Chihuahua. Then the Mex families down there would be eating free *gringo* beef until their *chicos* were grown up. The boss must have gone loco. But he was only a hired hand and orders were orders.

Long after Cole's trail dust had settled, Simpson was still on his porch watching his rifle-armed crew spill out of the bunkhouse to move away from the buildings to form a picket ring. He hard-smiled once more. He felt that he was getting into the position where he could call the moves, and win. See the bastards who were causing him all this trouble shot or strung up.

7

The nature of the high ground had changed dramatically, from grassy slopes to high black-faced bluffs and mesas. Ideal territory, Larribee opined, a natural one-move-ahead-thinking *hombre*, for hiding their back trail. He and Blaze were up on their mounts following the brothers, proudly carrying their newly come by rifles as they picked their way through the rock falls and shale slides. They had lost sight of the flames and smoke of the torched line cabin but still could see the faint dust haze of the herd they had sent high-tailing out of the draw they had been bedded down in.

Felix stopped and faced Larribee and Blaze. 'Through there, *señors*, is our camp!' he said, pointing to a narrow fissure in the rock face.

With only inches to spare the two *señors* guided their horses through a dark, narrow crack which didn't widen until they were several yards into the butte. Then there came some more twisting and turning until finally it opened out on a grass-covered clearing overshadowed by high bluffs. Larribee saw the rough, plank-built shack and the flames of a campfire and beyond the shack the glint of water. As a man regularly forced to go to ground, Larribee reckoned he couldn't have picked a safer, and more comfortable hole-up.

A quick look around gave him no sighting of the boys' grandfather. But both he and Blaze heard him. Least-ways they heard the ominous click of a rifle hammer being drawn back. Both of them spun round in their saddles to eyeball an old, grey-whiskered Mexican. Aged or not, he was holding the rifle steady enough. It was a long-barrelled, heavy-calibre weapon, as old as its owner, Larribee thought. And he judged that if the boys' grandpappy pulled the trigger it would blow one of them clear off his horse, and bring down a goodly piece of a butte's face.

It was Felix shouting frantically, 'They're *bueno amigos*, Grandfather! They saved my life! And are enemies of the dog Simpson!' that eased the situation for the pair.

'A *gringo* saved your life?' the old man gasped incredulously, still eyeing the 'life savers' suspiciously. He gave another gasp on seeing the rifles the boys were holding. 'You have fine Yankee rifles? How did you — ?'

'We have Yankee coffee and beans also,' a grinning Gomez put in.

'We took the supplies from the Yankee line cabin before we burnt it down,' Fierro added, his smile matching that of his brother. 'And we stampeded their cows!'

A muttered, '*Madre de Dios!*' was all that the bewildered old man could say.

Felix smiled. 'It was not the Mother of God who came to our aid, Grandfather, but our two *gringo compadres*.' Felix lost his smile. 'If Señor

Blaze had not wounded two of the Slash Y dogs I would now be hanging from a tree.'

The old Mexican shook his head, not taking in all the boys had told him, and of how near to death Felix had been. He gave another whispered, '*Madre de Dios*,' and lowered his rifle. 'Step down, *amigos*, and forgive an old peon's ill manners.' The two *amigos* breathed a sigh of relief.

'I am Villa. You're welcome to share the sparse comforts of my camp.' Villa managed a weak grin. 'Though thanks to you it is not so meagre. Felix, you and your brothers see to our *amigo's* horses, pronto, then bring wood for the fire!'

'*Muchas gracias, señor*,' Larribee said, and breathed a deep sigh of relief as he and Blaze dismounted. Old men with shaky trigger fingers scared him.

★ ★ ★

After they had eaten and while his two younger brothers were cleaning the plates and pans at the creek, Felix finished off relating to his grandfather all that had happened since the three of them had left the camp. Villa, only half listening, was eyeing the *gringo* enemies of the rancher Simpson. The young Señor Blaze had the quick, nervous all-seeing gaze of a *pistolero*, an *hombre* who sold his gun. *Hombres* who lived high and wild in the border towns here and along the Rio Bravo until they faced someone faster than them with a gun. Villa didn't think that Señor Larribee was a *pistolero* though he had the same watchful look. Maybe, he thought, the *señor* was a *bandido*. One thing he was sure of, Señor Larribee hadn't earned his keep by working for some *gringo* rancher. Whoever they were and the reason for their enmity against Simpson didn't matter. If they could keep his grandsons alive they were more than welcome at his fire.

Later on, when the boys had settled down for the night in the hut, Villa said that being he was an old *hombre* who didn't need much sleep he would stand the first watch at the head of the rocky passage. If he did feel tired he would wake up Felix to relieve him. Then their *gringo compadres* would be able to have an undisturbed night's sleep. It was an arrangement that suited Larribee: all the riding he had done since meeting up with Blaze was wearing him down.

* * *

Blaze, laying out his bedroll alongside Larribee's close to the fire, asked his partner if he'd come to some decision about allowing the brothers to join up with them in the fight against the Slash Y.

'It seems that we ain't got any other option, Blaze,' Larribee muttered. 'Those boys will be continuin' fightin' Simpson in their own way with or without our help, but I ain't happy about it. Me and you are only goin' to make Simpson

119

suffer by hittin' him where it hurts, in his pocket. The brothers, for a damn good reason, intend to kill Simpson. Now I may be a bank robber, an *hombre* who's always ridden outside the law, but I ain't a killer, paid or otherwise.' Glum-faced, he added, 'I've heard it said that Mr William Bonney and his crew would shoot down their first cousins and laugh doin' it, but, as I said, I ain't a born and bred killin' man.'

Blaze decided that, kid or not, it was time he spoke his mind. Like Billy he believed that there was only one rule to follow in a gun fight, shoot first and deadly true. He didn't want to rely on a partner who thought otherwise. 'I hope you don't think that it's uppity of me to give you some advice, to tell you that you worry too much.'

Larribee, red-faced with sudden anger, opened his mouth to tell Blaze to button his lip or he'd bend his Colt's pistol over his stupid cocky head, but Blaze silenced him with a raised hand.

'Hear me out first, Mr Larribee,' he

said. 'Then you can tell me that I ain't got the savvy to be your pard.'

Blaze took his partner's mumbled grunts as an OK for him to say his piece.

'What the hell's the use of worryin' about events when we don't know how they're goin' to turn out,' he began. 'By now Simpson could m'be have seen through our bluff and figured out that he ain't facin' a gang but just the two of us. But that ain't here or there, Mr Larribee; we were already marked men. Simpson is a stompin' man and he'll not get any satisfaction, until he sees us strung up. If it eases your feelin's any you ain't ridin' out to kill that rancher but to stop him and his boys killin' you.' Blaze cold-grinned. 'You're right about one thing, partner: Billy would have killed those three Slash Y men; he don't believe in wastin' shells just wingin' *hombres*. And I'll tell you this, I'm sidin' with the brothers. If I get Simpson framed in my rifle sights the bastard's dead!' Blaze waited nervously

121

for the angry reply from the man he was beholden to.

Larribee had enough chewing away at his guts without having a stand-up argument with Blaze; he needed his handiness with his guns. And whether or not he liked it the boy was speaking the truth. He resigned himself to the unpleasant fact that the only help he was going to get in the fight against the Slash Y were the brothers and old Villa. He gave a silent snort. And Blaze reckoned he worried too much.

'Pard,' he said. 'I get your drift. Now, if you've finished speechifying I'd like to get some sleep; we've got some dangerously busy days ahead of us. And just for the record I'll willingly shoot down any bastard who throws down on me, OK?'

'I never doubted that, *amigo*,' replied an inner smiling Blaze, as he lay down on his bedroll, greatly pleased that he and the old worrier were still pards.

★ ★ ★

122

Night was well set in when Jack was on his way back to the ranch. His trip to San Remo to find out the whereabouts of the kid shootist and his pard had been fruitless, as he knew it would be, but when Simpson said jump a hired hand had to do just that or lose his job. Burgess, the *cantina* owner, had told him that the men who had killed Bull and crippled Caleb must be in Arizona.

'It stands to reason,' he had said. 'They'd be loco if they stayed within forty miles of the Slash Y after the shootin'.'

'The kid was in Arizona, Burgess,' Jack said. 'He roughed up a couple of the boys in a saloon in Boulder Rock for no reason at all, or so the boys said.'

'Jeez,' Burgess gasped. 'It seems to me that the two *pistoleros* have a long-standing grievance with old man Simpson and are kinda levellin' up the score.'

'I reckon Simpson is feelin' that way,' replied Jack. 'That's why he's sent me here, on a goddamned wild goose chase on the off chance that the bastards have returned to San Remo. He's even told me to ask the Mex farmers if they've seen them ridin' around.'

Burgess burst out laughing. 'You're wastin' your time, Jack. Those greaser farmers wouldn't give your boss the time of day let alone information about a coupla *gringos* who have some sort of killin' dispute with the Slash Y, not when his wild-assed drovers drive the longhorns across their cornfields and vegetable patches and laugh about it as though it was some great joke. Sit down and have a coupla drinks on the house before you ride back then you won't have hard-assed it all the way here for damn all. We can talk about the old days when San Remo was a wide open town.'

Jack sat down. He was willing to talk about the old days, or any other day, as long as the whiskeys kept coming across.

★ ★ ★

Seeing a string of small fires cutting across the home range had Jack puzzled. His whiskey-fuddled mind had him thinking that he was once more soldiering with General Shelby riding through a Confederate picket line after a successful raid against a blue-belly encampment.

Someone shouting out, 'Is that you, Jack?' cleared his thinking somewhat, and alarmed him. What was the reason for the pickets, he wondered. It couldn't be that there was a Comanche horse-lifting party roaming here-abouts. There had been no Indian trouble on the Slash Y land for years. It could only mean one thing: the two shootists were a lot nearer to the home range than Arizona. He belatedly wished that he'd refused Burgess's offer of talking about the old days, and the drinks, then he could have reached the ranch in the daylight.

'Yeah, it's me!' he yelled back, then glanced nervously about him. It was still a fair ride to the bunkhouse and it was pitch black beyond the flickering flames of the fires, dark enough for two bold, pistol-wielding sons-of-bitches, who had it in for Simpson and the Slash Y, to put paid to him. It was a rapidly sobering up Jack who rib-kicked his mount into a gallop for the safety of the bunkhouse walls.

8

Jim Crow was up on the ridge gazing down at the charred remains of the line cabin, going over in his mind the reading of the tracks he had picked up at the cabin and here on the ridge. Finally, he reckoned, he hadn't let down his dead Comanche pa, he'd read the signs right. There had only been two riders, the deadly shooting kid and the old man who rode with him, and three sets of footprints. The bastards had fooled Butler into thinking there had been a whole bunch of them.

Jim Crow mounted up and came down on to the flat by the same faint trace of a track the two *gringos* had used and discovered that they were travelling with the Mex boys and by now must be in their hide-out. A place he was determined to find to further his pride as a tracker equal to a full-blood

127

Comanche. He had offered to track down the kids when they first started to steal Slash Y cows, but Simpson had told him that he wouldn't take men off their regular ranch chores just to stop the odd longhorn being lifted.

'Those greaser kids will get careless,' he had said. 'One day they'll run slap bang into some of the boys ridin' the herd then we'll have ourselves a hanging.'

But they hadn't been roped in, Jim Crow thought, and now they'd got themselves a couple of Yankee hard men who, for some reason or other, were keen to gun down Slash Y ranch hands.

He could ride back to tell Simpson how he had read things but he had no doubts that when the rancher knew that only two men did the shooting he would have every man on the ranch raising the dust in trying to find the Mexicans' camp. The Mexicans weren't blind; they would soon spot that there were men out in force seeking them out and move deeper into the hills. His first plan was the best: find their bolt hole then sneak up on the camp. Jim Crow smiled, Indian style, as his pa would have done. Catch them off guard enabling him to gun down the two *gringos*. Though he guessed that Simpson would want him to take them alive so he could question them about why they were shooting down his men, before he strung them up. He would have to see how it panned out when he found the camp. Once on the flat he swung down from his horse again to pick up the trail.

After an hour's painstaking eyeballing the occasional upturned rock, the mark of a rope sandal in a stretch of dust between the boulders, Jim Crow straightened up. He had lost the tracks, though not his gut feeling that he was close to the hidden camp. Ahead of him the bluffs rose steep and broken-faced and within a hundred yards or so were two cracks which, he believed, could open up into small box canyons deep in the buttes.

Jim Crow led his mount in the shade of an overhanging rock ledge. It could be a long, hot vigil until it became dark enough for him to scout around without being seen by any lookout the raiders had posted.

To his surprise he hadn't to wait as long as he had been prepared to do. He saw a young boy holding a rifle suddenly appear in his sight as though he had sprung from out of the butte face. His hunch had paid off; he had found the Mexicans' camp. He smiled again, and had also found a way into the camp with the edge in his favour.

Gomez, with the impatient eagerness of youth, had come out into the open well clear of the lookout post. He knew that yesterday's shootings and the destruction of the line cabin, as well as stampeding the herd, had stepped up their fight against Simpson into a real kill or be killed struggle, which both excited and scared him. The *gringo* rancher would have raised up a great hunt for him and his brothers and their *gringo compadres*, yet he could not see any dust trails of riders criss-crossing the plain seeking them out.

Gomez heard a slight scraping noise behind him. Alarmed, he gripped his rifle with both hands and made to swing round. A rifle muzzle digging painfully in the small of his back stilled his movement.

'You just let go of that rifle, *chico*,' he heard a harsh voice order, 'or I'll blow a hole through you!'

Gomez gave a low cry of pain as the rifle dug in his flesh again. His rifle dropped from nerveless fingers and clattered noisily on the rocks. The vendetta against Simpson was no longer exciting, only frightening. And worse. His foolish action by coming out into the open had endangered everyone at the camp.

'*Bueno*,' said Jim Crow. 'Now we'll head back to whatever crack in the rocks you came out of.' He gave his prisoner another jab with his rifle. 'Nice and quiet like.'

Gomez risked a quick glance over his shoulder and glimpsed a stone-eyed face. Dejectedly he began to walk towards the entrance to the camp, chivvied along by the rifle of the man he took to be part Indian. He thought of yelling out a warning before they reached the opening; he was beholden to do so, but, to his shame, his fear of being killed had dried up his throat.

The *compadres* at the fire — the *gringos* finishing off their coffees, the brothers cleaning their rifles — didn't know the danger they were in until Jim Crow stepped into view from behind Gomez with his rifle pressed into Gomez's side. Then it was too late for any of them to do anything.

'I'm holdin' an eight-shot Spencer,' Jim Crow said conversationally. 'So I'd ponder well if any of you are thinkin' of makin' a fight of it. Before you can bring your guns into play I'll have pulled off three loads. One each for you two *gringos*, the other for the kid here.' Jim Crow bared his teeth in a wolfish grin. 'I'll back shoot those two kids while they're runnin' scared.' Jim Crow took up the first pressure on the trigger, and close watched the two *gringos*, the dangerous *hombres*.

Larribee saw Blaze's gun hand twitch. 'Stay put!' he hissed. 'The sonuvabitch has us by the balls!'

Which Larribee thought wasn't quite true. By the Slash Y man's cocky look he was thinking that he had the drop on every man in the camp. He didn't know that the kids had a grandpappy. The old man was inside the shack having his siesta. Though it was a wild hope, Villa could wake up, suss what was going on, and cut loose with his small cannon. It was more than likely that Villa would stagger out still half asleep and that would start a shooting hell.

'You two kids put your rifles down and get on to your feet,' Jim Crow said. 'Grab hold of that coil of rope lyin' there against the side of the shack and hogtie those two Yankees. No fancy tricks, or your brother gets dead.'

Felix and Fierro laid down their rifles and got to their feet and walked across to pick up the rope, neither of them making a sudden move that would cause the death of Gomez.

Jim Crow shot a look at the younger of the two *gringos*. He didn't need his father's blood to recognize the killing lust on the *gringo*'s face. The young *pistolero* was itching to pull out his gun.

'I don't like the look you're givin' me, *gringo*,' he snarled. 'So I'll save Mr Simpson a length of rope.' He brought his rifle away from Gomez and drew a bead on Blaze.

The roaring bark of Villa's gun fired from inside the doorway of the shack, its blast shattering most of the front of the shack, echoed around the canyon like a roll of thunder. The heavy, rough-cast ball tore away the right side of Jim Crow's face in a bloody welter of flesh and bone, hurling him backwards as though he had been struck by a sudden gust of wind. A blood-spattered

Gomez pissed himself.

Larribee and Blaze sprang to their feet, hands grabbing for their rifles, Larribee issuing sharp-voiced orders.

'Get along that cuttin', Blaze!' he said. 'See if there's any more of the sonsuvbitches hangin' around. I don't think there'll be, or they would have come in with that fella lyin' there, but that shot musta been heard clear to San Remo. You go with him, Felix. Fierro, take Gomez down to the crick and clean him up. Then both of you gather up what bits and pieces you've got; we don't want this place to be a death trap!'

Blaze, mad-eyed, more with having been thrown down on than almost being shot, ran across to the opening of the rocky defile. He hoped that there were Slash Y men out there — the Death Shadow was hovering over him.

Felix hadn't moved. He was still deciding whether he should help Fierro with the petrified-looking Gomez or carry out Señor Larribee's orders.

'Vamoose, Felix, pronto,' Villa said, as he came out of the shack. 'Do as the *señor* says before the camp is overrun by men seeking our blood!'

Felix gave a mumbled, '*Sí*, Grandfather!' and, picking up his rifle, hurried after Blaze, eager to use his new rifle to protect what was left of his family, and to prove to the *pistolero*, Señor Blaze, he had the courage to stand alongside him.

'You got us out of one hell of a situation, *amigo*,' Larribee said to Villa, as the old man stepped up to the fire. 'That Slash Y man was just about to send my pard to an early grave.'

'I heard his threats, Señor Larribee,' replied Villa, 'but had to wait until the dog took his rifle off Gomez before I could fire,' he added, almost apologetically.

'You shot true, friend,' Larribee said. 'And that's all that matters.' He cast an apprehensive look at the opening in the rock before asking Villa if there was a back way out of the canyon. 'A trail that horses can manage, so they can carry whatever you've got here. And being that I ain't much of a walker.'

Villa smiled. 'Do not worry, *amigo*. There is a trail that leads out of here and with care its passable for horses.'

Villa crossed to where the dead Jim Crow lay and, putting down his old rifle, picked up the Spencer. He hefted it, feeling the balance of the gun. He sighed then grinned at Larribee. 'It's the finest rifle I have ever owned.'

'You couldn't have shot that fella any deader with it than you did with your old gun,' Larribee said. 'Take his pistol and gun-belt as well; he won't need them where he is now that's for sure.' Then he got back to fretting again.

It had been over fifteen minutes since Blaze and Felix had left on their scouting mission and there had been no sounds of gunfire. That could be a good sign, he thought, but it didn't ease his worrying any. Fierro and Gomez, somewhat recovered from his fearful ordeal, had saddled up the two horses and loaded them with what few possessions there were in the camp. Now they stood in a tight, grim-faced group, all loaded for bear.

It was a wide-grinning Blaze who came back into the canyon, closely followed by Felix rein-leading a saddle horse.

'He's the only one, Mr Larribee! There ain't another Slash Y rider in sight. That's his horse Felix is leadin' in!'

Then it was smiles all round as the tension eased. They had won another skirmish in the war against the Slash Y. They began to unload the horses.

'I got things wrong, Blaze,' Larribee admitted. 'I thought that all the trouble we sicced on Simpson yesterday would have him mad enough to ride out with all his boys and try and track us down. Then while their noses were stuck to the ground lookin' for sign, we could've swung by them and done some damage on his home range.'

'Simpson didn't get where he is by

makin' too many mistakes, Mr Larribee,' Blaze said. 'That man you put down, Señor Villa, had the look of a mixed blood man, before you blew his face away. I reckon he was part Injun and was sent out by Simpson to find this camp. Once he'd done that he would report back to Simpson, then the whole Slash Y crew could have come thunderin' along that defile.'

'That means we've still got the edge,' a brightening-up Larribee said. 'We know where most of his boys are but he don't know where we are. If we send that 'breed back Simpson will know that we're still in business. Tryin' to swallow the death of another one of his men could force him to change his plans, bring out his men on the wild chance he can track us down. What I banked on him doin'. So we can still maybe get the chance to torch Mr Simpson's fine house.'

Larribee gave his small band of fighters a wry grin. 'I know it ain't much of a plan, *amigos*, but we're forced to hit hard and fast, whenever we get the chance We ain't got the supplies or the ammunition for a long-standin' fight with a whole ranch crew.'

Larribee looked at Villa and asked him if he had any misgivings about his grandsons wanting to take part in the attack on the ranch house. Larribee could see by the boys' determined, eager looks that they wanted to be in at the kill with their *gringo compadres*.

Villa smiled resignedly. '*Amigo*, I have given up a long time ago to tell my grandsons what they should or should not do. The Indians have a belief that a man's future is all written out in his book of life.' Villa's eyes flashed in deep-rooted anger. 'They're fated to hunt down the *gringos* who butchered their parents. They will try to do that with or without your help, Señor Larribee. I would worry less if they had you and Señor Blaze's guns to aid them. They are *hombres* now; their pride won't allow them to let you down, Señor Larribee,' Villa added almost pleadingly.

'I hope that the three *hombres* will allow two *gringos* to help them to get their revenge, Señor Villa,' a slightly smiling Larribee replied. 'Now let's get that fella slung across his horse and sent on his way before he starts to smell. And you three *hombres* fix up your grandpappy's shack, or you're goin' to have a draughty night's sleep. I want you up early, fresh and clear-eyed, ready to look out across the plain for any signs of riders. Remember we can only move when Simpson decides to move.'

Larribee watched the boys chatting and smiling at each other as they walked down to the creek to gather up some brushwood to patch up the shack, not seemingly to be giving a hoot that they could be dead this time tomorrow. That sombre thought got him thinking of what could be scribed in that book old Villa spoke of about Mr Jake

Larribee's and Mr Blaze Morgan's futures. It didn't need an Indian shaman to tell him that they definitely had, like the Mexican boys, a very uncertain future.

9

There was a thin line of lookouts ringing the ranch building. The night pickets were in the bunkhouse, sleeping with their boots on, their horses tied up outside ready to ride out at a minute's notice.

Pete Drummond could see Simpson striding back and forth along the porch of the ranch house and thought that his boss would wear a hole in the planking if Jim Crow didn't show up soon; the 'breed had been out over four hours. And he'd better come in with some good news or the boss would plug him out of hand just to ease his anger. He would do likewise if Jim Crow couldn't put him on the trail of the killers of his brother. A lookout's yell of, 'Rider comin' in!' had him picking up his rifle and walking across to the house with blood-shedding anticipation.

Simpson stopped his pacing on hearing the shout and leaned over the porch rails having the same expectations as his new straw boss. He gave Drummond a fierce twist of a grin as he stepped on to the porch.

'We're goin' to see those sonsuvbitches hang, Pete!' he said. 'You can have the pleasure of slipping the noose over that kid *pistolero's* neck!'

A further yell of, 'It's Jim Crow's horse but he ain't in the saddle! He's lyin' across its back!' put an abrupt end to their confident thoughts of having a hanging party, as they quickly realized that Jim Crow was not the bringer of good news, or any other news, ever.

A pale-faced ranch hand led the horse and its grisly load up to the house and Simpson and Drummond got a close look at Jim Crow's fearful head wound.

'Jesus Christ!' gasped a shocked Simpson. 'What gun did the sonsuvbitches use to do that to Jim Crow, Pete? A shotgun?'

'Naw, boss,' replied Drummond, as blood-drained-faced as the ranch hand holding the horse's reins. 'He was shot at close range by a heavy calibre rifle, m'be a .50 Sharps' buffalo gun. Damn close,' he added under his breath. Pete was worried more than somewhat. The two shootists were sneaky enough to get the drop on a part Indian and while he had a great natural urge to avenge the killing of his brother it could be a fatal mistake to go mad-assed after the two gunmen, or he could end up with half a face like poor Jim Crow. Seeing Simpson's crazy-eyed look didn't give him any comfort. His boss's stomped on pride wanted blood, and pronto.

Yet when Simpson told the ranch hand to see to it that Jim Crow was decently buried and to get some of the crew to help him, his voice was calm and matter of fact. Pete reckoned that Simpson had also realized that he had to be smarter than the men they were trying to track down.

'Pete,' Simpson said, his voice still

flat and expressionless, though Pete could see the craziness at the back of his eyes. 'Roust the boys out of the bunkhouse; we move out in ten minutes. Leave the men standing watch at their posts; the bastards ain't strong enough to attack this place in daylight and we'll be back before nightfall.'

'Where are we ridin' to, boss?' Pete asked, thinking that they'd be riding up their own asses as no other hand had the tracking skills of the late Jim Crow.

'We're goin' to pay a call on those Mex sodbusters and sheep herders,' Simpson replied. 'According to Jack they've no idea where those Mex kids and their Yankee *amigos* are holed-up.' The rancher gave another one of his snarling smiles. 'M'be Jack didn't ask them hard enough, like I intend to do.'

Pete grinned. The boss was using his brains. Then he thought of how accommodating that pretty Mexican 'breed girl would be to stop him from beating up her pa again.

'I'll get the boys outa their bunks,

boss,' he said, 'and put Clem in charge of the ranch pickets.' He hurried across to the cookhouse and picked up the iron bar striker and rattled it with some force against the 'chow up' triangle. His shouts of 'Rouse yourselves, boys! The boss wants you up on your horses and movin' out in ten minutes. We're goin' visitin'!' sounded above the clanging of the triangle.

★　★　★

Amos Brewster sat huddled up in a chair on the veranda of his late wife's sister's *hacienda*. Though now he could move around with the use of only one stick, albeit slowly, from the beating Pete Drummond had given him, the burning down of his store, his daughter's future dowry, still cut hard in him, putting him into a dark, despondent mood, causing Carla to be sick with worry for him.

An added worry for Carla was the well-being of the young *pistolero*,

147

Blaze, and his *compadre*, Señor Larribee. She shuddered with horror when she thought of what her fate would have been if Blaze had not risked his life and killed her ravisher.

Carla sniffed back her tears as she blamed herself for all the pain and loss her father had suffered. If only she had come here to Aunt Sofia's when her father had first suggested it none of this trouble would have happened. And what if the Slash Y men caught up with the two *compadres*? Her hands flew to her lips to stifle the horrified gasp. She would be responsible for two unnecessary deaths. Then Carla could no longer hold back her tears. Her sobs came heavy and body racking.

10

All the *compadres*, with the exception of old Villa, were out in the open well clear of the bluffs, eagle-eying the far reaches of the plain for signs of their hunters that would mean Larribee's wild gamble was beginning to work. The last dead ranch hand had riled Simpson enough for him to come out with his men to track them down.

The second part of Larribee's plan depended on Felix guiding them along the the beds of arroyos and dry washes which would enable them to swing round any hunters unseen until they were within striking range of the Slash Y. Then, chance that Simpson would have only left a skeleton crew to protect the ranch reasoning that two men and three Mex boys wouldn't be crazy enough to launch an attack on his ranch in daylight hours.

If things at the ranch were as favourable as Larribee hoped, the three brothers would crawl in close and with great speed, brush-boy fashion, put a torch to the big house. Then pull out under the covering fire of Larribee and Blaze's rifles.

Larribee had a further hope that having his fine house burnt down and some of his crew killed or badly shot up, Simpson would quit raising cows in this section of New Mexico and move on, ending the need for Villa and his grandsons to continue their vendetta against him, and saving their lives and, more than likely, his and Blaze's as well.

Larribee was chewing nervously at his lower lip. Why hadn't the bastards shown up? The Slash Y crew must be mad as hell having their buddies shot dead and would be wondering if they were the next candidates for a wooden box. They would need no pleading from Simpson to ride on the vengeance trail. It had been over three hours since he'd slapped the flanks of the horse to send

150

it trotting on its way where it knew it would find grain with its dead rider laid across the saddle. The more he thought about the planned raid the more loco it seemed and odds on to get them all killed, to leave old Villa to keep up the fight against the Slash Y until he paid the full penalty for his pride by getting himself shot, or strung up. Not for the first time Larribee regretted he had ridden south.

The long waiting for action was playing hell with Blaze's nerves. When he had ridden with Billy and the boys any worrying he had only lasted as long as it took him to buckle on his gunbelt, mount up, and gun down whoever it was who had caused him the upset. This time it was different; he couldn't get at the men who were causing the churning in his guts. He glanced across at Larribee and noticed that his normally po-faced partner had a strained look about him. Blaze gave a twitch of a grin But then he had discovered that Mr Larribee was a natural born worrying *hombre*. Blaze's face twisted into a scowl, he'd had a bellyful of this waiting game and thought it was time he told that to his partner. He shifted close to Larribee before speaking.

'I got a feelin' we're wastin' our time sittin' here on our asses,' he said. 'Simpson and his crew ain't about to show up. The sonsuvbitches could be forted-up at the ranch shakin' in their boots thinkin' that two men and three kids are about to come ridin' in shootin' and a hollerin'! But I don't think so. Simpson and his boys are out huntin' for us.' He gimlet-eyed Larribee. 'But why not here, Mr Larribee, where he knows we've been seen? The bastard's out-foxed us!' Then Blaze did some lip chewing of his own trying to think of what Simpson's tactics were.

'The not showin' up of Simpson has me wonderin', Blaze,' Larribee replied. 'He oughta be chasin' us, not us trackin' him. The sonuvabitch must have a plan of his own!'

'There's only one way to find out if Simpson's still at the Slash Y,' Blaze said. 'Me and Felix could go and check out the ranch. See what's goin' on there.'

Larribee gave his partner a calculating look. The kid was right, they couldn't sit on their asses all day waiting and wondering about Simpson's probable tactics.

His face steeled over. 'But make it just a looksee, Blaze,' he warned. 'Then report back here, pronto, *comprende*? I don't want Felix killed by any mad-ass move on your part. The boy ain't as slick with a gun as your old *compadres* up there in Lincoln County are.'

'Just a looksee it is, Mr Larribee,' Blaze replied. 'I ain't no Billy the Kid.'

'You'll need to go on your scout on foot,' Larribee said. 'You might be forced to do some quick movin' around.' The tension in his face eased into a slight smile. 'But by the time you've covered the four, five miles to the Slash Y wearing spurred boots you'll only be able to hobble around. Ask old Villa if he's got a spare pair of sandals.'

Blaze flashed a beaming grin. 'I'm on my way, pard.' He was harbouring a great urge to shoot some Slash Y men and would walk to the ranch in his stockinged feet rather than sit here in the baking sun being eaten alive by flying bugs.

★   ★   ★

'Down, Felix, down!' Blaze whispered sharply. 'I got a smell of cigarillo smoke.' A nerve-jangling Felix ate dirt alongside Blaze in the high-growing buffalo grass at the foot of a slight rolling rise.

Their passage had taken well over an hour, stumbling along the rocky beds of dry gullies and washes, jumping scared as they disturbed sleeping rattlers, until at last, sweating and dry-throated, they scrambled out of a wash that Felix told Blaze cut away from the Slash Y ranch.

From now on in it would mean moving across open ground, though land with tall yellow buffalo grass and patches of brush growing on it which meant that the way to their goal was still in the two *compadres*' favour.

After twenty minutes of spurts of low crouching running, the pair dropped flat to the ground at the foot of a low grassy ridge to get their breath back. It gave time for Felix to brace himself for the scramble up to the crest from where they would have a clear view of the ranch house, and the frightening possibility that they could end up dead in a gunfight with the Slash Y crew.

Blaze, more settled-nerved, having come through unharmed from many suchlike situations, was casting a keen-eyed gaze every which way for the man smoking a cigarillo the strong tangy smoke of which he'd just caught a smell, but he couldn't see, nor hear anyone moving about. He figured that the unseen smoker must be one of the guards Simpson would have prowling close to his main buildings and who had moved further along his beat. He didn't tell Felix about the picket, not wanting to worry him more than he must be right now. Instead, he gave Felix a fake confident grin, nodded towards the rimline and began belly-crawling uphill. Felix followed him with his rifle almost slipping out of hands greasy with sweat, much of it raised by the fear that he could, when the moment of truth came, lack the courage to stand bold, at the *pistolero* Blaze's side.

'There are only three men down there, Señor Blaze!' Felix gasped in surprise.

By the number of horses in the corral Blaze reckoned that there must be another four or so men behind them as lookouts.

Blaze, not wanting Felix to think him a foul-mouthed *hombre*, swore under his breath.

'It's as Señor Larribee feared,' he said. 'That sonuvabitch, Simpson, has a plan of his own and he's out there somewhere with most of his crew carryin' it out.'

Angry at being outfoxed, Blaze took a longer look at the house and barns and the position of the ranch hands busy with their chores. He opined that it wouldn't take long to come down off the ridge and by using the barns as cover get close enough to put Simpson's fine built house to the torch. And in the uproar the burning building would create, get to hell out of it fast. Though remembering his partner's warning, the burning down of the house had to remain a disappointing thought.

'OK, Felix,' he finally said. 'Let's get back to the camp and tell Señor Larribee the bad news. M'be he'll be able to figure out what Simpson's up to.'

With Blaze leading they had come down from the ridge and had made no more than a few yards to the shelter of the wash when Blaze met up with the cigarillo smoker, a Slash Y hand stepping out of a patch of brush slipping his suspenders back over his shoulders.

Blaze got over the surprise encounter first and swung up his rifle for a killing shot, knowing the brutal fact that the sound of a gunshot would bring Slash Y men from every direction. As his finger tightened on the trigger something sun-glinting hissed past his head. Then Blaze heard the sickening thud of a heavy-bladed knife striking human flesh and saw the Slash Y man fling out his arms and fall backwards into the brush.

Blaze swung round and gave Felix a congratulatory grin. 'You did well, *compadre*,' he said. 'If I had to pull off a load this place would have been like an overturned hornets' nest with us slap-bang in the middle of it. Now let's head home; they'll be worryin' about us.' He gave another grin. 'And before we bump into any more of the Slash Y crew taken short.'

Felix, tasting the bitterness of bile at

the back of his throat at his first killing, didn't feel like going anywhere, he just wanted to throw up. Then the praise from a genuine *pistolero* who had killed many *hombres* sank in; settled down his stomach, made him feel a real *hombre*. Even allowing him to force out a small smile as he thought of how he would have something to tell his grandfather and brothers when they made it back to the camp. With one last look at the brush where his first kill lay hidden, he slid down into the wash.

11

As impassive-faced as a full-blood Indian, Larribee eyed the nearby arroyo willing Blaze and Felix to come climbing over its rim. Fierro and Gomez were also doing some scouting north of the camp where the cabin had been burned down hoping they could pick up the trail of the Slash Y men. Hunters — Larribee's guts and every other sense were telling him, though he had never seen so much as a wisp of their trail dust — were out there searching for them. His small army was now scattered all over the territory.

He'd just had a cup of coffee at the camp and was returning to take over the watch from old Villa when he saw him and the two boys having a heated argument. He couldn't understand much Mexican but by the pointing of the boys' arms northwards he guessed that they weren't prepared to sit on their asses any longer; like Felix, they wanted to be in the action. Villa told him just that when he came up to them.

'I tried to tell the *muchachos*,' Villa continued, 'that you were the *hombre* who gave out the orders.'

And not liking it, Larribee thought sourly, but he wasn't about to stop the boys from doing what they felt honour bound to do. 'You two can go out on your scout, if your grandfather OKs it.' His voice hardened. 'But as I told your brother and Señor Blaze, scoutin' only, *comprende*? If you see so much as those Slash Y riders' trail dust you haul your asses back here, pronto like.'

'*Sí*, Señor Larribee,' the wide-grinning boys replied in unison. They looked across pleadingly at their grandfather. Old Villa nodded his permission and the two brothers dashed back to the camp to pick up their reload belts.

Larribee wanted to tell Villa that not since he had charged shouting and cheering with the rest of General

Hood's Texicans at the blue-belly lines on Cemetery Ridge had he seen boys so keen to get themselves killed, but he had the savvy to keep his feelings to himself realizing that the old man must be having the same kind of morbid thoughts, thoughts a man needed to ponder over on his own.

'Go and get yourself some coffee while it's still hot,' he said soft-voiced. 'I'll let you know when Felix and Blaze show up.'

* * *

In between close-watching the arroyo, Larribee was doing some heavy thinking of his own. Of how a man's life could change completely by events he'd no control of. A week or so ago he was living it up with enough wherewithal to pay for the services of a hot-blooded female, rubbing shoulders with men at some bar who weren't itching to gun him down. To cap it all he was looking forward to robbing a bank, the safe of which was bulging with cash. And now here he was fretting over four boys as though he was their pa in the thick of what was turning out to be a range war, such as was being played out in Lincoln County. Though up there, he thought gloomily, the two factions were evenly matched. He gave a derisive sniff. Bill Bonney and his Boys wouldn't come amiss right now, on his side.

★　★　★

Simpson, leaning across his saddle horn, gimlet-eyed the Mexican family standing in front of their shack; the man of the house, with his quietly sobbing woman clinging to him; and an almost grown up boy. In a quiet tone of voice that belied his blood-chilling gaze he said, 'A day or so ago one of my men came by this way asking you Mexican famers and sheepmen if they had seen any sightings of two *gringo pistoleros* hereabouts but he got no joy.' Simpson straightened up in his saddle. 'Now I'm here to ask you the same question.' His voice now held the menace his gaze had. 'They're running with those three Mexican kids who've been lifting my stock; now the sonsuvbitches are gunning down my men. I'm hoping you'll appreciate how my boys are feeling having to bury their *amigos* and that you'll be more forthcoming with information this time.'

Señor Castro's blood chilled as he took in the expressions of the *gringo* rancher's 'boys'. Some were of his race, *vaqueros*, but they were as merciless-visaged as their *gringo compadres*. He prayed that his son, Antonio, wouldn't do anything rash such as threatening the Slash Y hard men with the broad-bladed, cane-cutting knife he was still holding. Rumours of how rancher Simpson was having bad trouble had reached the outlying Mexican communities and was welcome news. The rancher had been encroaching on more and more of their land and water as he built up his herd. He was also pleased to hear that Villa's grandsons had the guns of the *gringo pistoleros* to aid them in their fight against the killers of their parents.

Castro swallowed hard and tried not to show his family the fear he felt. Simpson hadn't ridden here with most of his men just to ask him a question.

'I have not seen the two *gringos* you spoke of, Señor Simpson. And as for the Mexican boys, all I know is they live with their grandfather somewhere in the Black Ridge badlands. I swear by the Holy *Madre* I speak the truth, *señor!*'

Simpson sighed. He didn't doubt that the farmer was speaking the truth; he looked too fightened to lie but he had to throw a scare in all the Mexican farmers whose holdings lay along the western edge of the Slash Y. His plan was to make sure that they knew, pronto, of the destruction of this farmer's crops, and the reason why.

Simpson wasn't about to lead his men into a fire-raising sweep along the valley as General Sherman had done on his bloody march through Georgia during the war. He hadn't the men, or the time, to grind to dust every Mexican farmer's crops. And if he had, such would be the outcry of the farmers, he would have the state governor sending in US marshals or a detachment of troops and the Slash Y ranch would be no more. He was gambling he could get away destroying one farmer's livelihood by claiming that the farmer and his boy were caught stealing his cows.

The implied threat that they would suffer the same fate would put the fear of God into the other farmers and one of them would crack and give him the information he was seeking. Simpson was a firm believer in blood being thicker than water which meant that someone in the Mexican community was aiding the Mexican brothers in their fight against the *gringo* rancher.

He gave Drummond a curt nod. Drummond grinned and gave a nod of his own and six riders peeled off the bunch and rode at a trot to the nearby field of high standing corn.

'No, señor, no!' a horrified Castro screamed. 'It's winter food for my family!' He broke free of his wife's grip and made to chase after the riders. The ominous snicking of rifle hammers being thumbed back stayed his wild dash. Antonio, loco with anger, ignored the cocked rifles and hurled himself at the nearest Slash Y rider his cane knife raised high. The ranch hand, mindful of his boss's orders that there hadn't to be any shooting unless the situation was swinging away from them, leaned sideways and laid his rifle barrel hard against Antonio's head that partly stunned him. Antonio, blood streaming down his brow, swayed drunkenly on his legs, his machete lying on the ground by his feet.

'I saved you from being shot, boy,' Simpson said, 'because I want you to get up on that old horse you've got hitched up outside the barn and ride to your nearest neighbours and let them know what's happened here and make sure that you tell them why. *Comprende*? Also, tell them that me and my crew will be calling on them next to ask the same questions. Now get riding!'

In spite of his painfully throbbing head, Antonio still had the anger and hate in him to scowl up at the rancher before casting his father a, 'what shall I do?' glance.

'Come, boy,' Castro said. 'I will help you with the saddle.' He strode over to his son and put a steadying hand on his shoulder as they walked across to the horse.

'Keep an eye on them, Luke,' Simpson told the ranch hand who had clubbed Antonio. 'Though it seems that they've lost the fire to cause us any trouble.'

Luke pulled his mount round and followed the pair with his slow-stepping horse, too far behind them to hear Castro whisper to his son, 'Ride first to Señora Sofia's *hacienda* where Señor

Brewster and his daughter are staying. Tell the sutler to go south, to Mexico, with his daughter before Simpson and the dogs who run with him ride in to question him again.'

Like all the Mexicans in the valley Castro knew of the shooting of Bull Drummond, and the near rape of Carla Brewster by Pete Drummond, then Brewster's beating up and the burning down of his store. Simpson was seeking answers by any means and what a young *señorita* could suffer at the hands of the animals, whose horses had flattened his corn chilled Castro's blood.

Castro helped his son into his saddle and handed him the reins. Antonio swayed slightly and an anxious Castro asked if he was OK.

'I'm OK, Father,' Antonio replied, firm-voiced. 'The *señor* and his daughter will be warned.'

As he watched his boy ride out Castro heaped curses on Simpson and his men. In the matter of a few minutes

169

he had lost a year's crop and almost lost a son. It was a bow-backed, broken-spirited *hombre* who walked back to his shack to comfort his distraught wife.

Pete Drummond led the way out of the hoof-churned dust bowl of a cornfield to join up with Simpson and the rest of the crew. He wondered how many cornfields would have to be destroyed before his boss's gamble paid off. Being a natural born taking man, Drummond didn't have any pangs of conscience destroying the Mexicans' growing lands but he was worried about his own skin. Pushing the Mexican farmers too hard could force them to band together to protect themselves. Outgun them if it came to a face to face shoot-out. Unless, he thought hopefully, his boss acted on his suggestion.

'It's done, boss,' he said, as he drew his horse up alongside Simpson. 'That greaser sodbuster won't see any corn growin' in that field till next summer.' He grinned wolfishly. 'It'll be a hungry winter for him and his family.'

Simpson replied with a savage snarled, 'Let's move out and see if the next farmer has taken heed of my message and is willing to talk to us.' His grand dream of being accepted by the Mexicans in the valley as the *gringo* cattle don of the south-west had been shattered. But he had to weigh that disappointment with the loss of face he was suffering by not being able to prevent three ragged-ass Mexican boys and two Yankee drifters gunning down his men.

'M'be we oughta have another talk with the sutler, boss,' Drummond said tentatively, not knowing if Simpson didn't like the way his thinking had changed. 'I've a feelin' that storekeeper didn't tell us all he knew about those two sonsuvbitches.'

Simpson cold-eyed his straw boss. He was also having feelings. Feelings that while Drummond was wanting revenge for the killing of his brother he also wanted to try and get his paws on the sutler's pretty daughter again. So be it,

171

he thought, iron-hearted. The gloves were off. Folk were going to get hurt or threatened until the two gunmen were swinging from some tree. He wasn't about to let the Mexican farmers and sheepherders, no lovers of *gringo* cattlemen, to mock him behind his back for failing to stop the raids against the Slash Y.

'While it could be worth our while to check out the sutler again,' replied Simpson. 'We haven't got the time to ride halfway to the border to find out who the storekeeper's staying with.'

Drummond grinned. 'He's stayin' with kinfolk at a run down *hacienda* on the main trail to the Mexican border, not more than a half-hour's ride from this place.' Seeing Simpson's doubting look he said, 'It's true, boss. Sancho there, has just told me that he'd heard from a cousin of his who tends sheep in that section of the territory that he'd seen the sutler and his daughter at the *hacienda*.'

Simpson didn't think too long about

his straw boss's suggestion. The storekeeper and his daughter had had the closest contact with the two gunmen. Maybe the pair had mentioned to the sutler their grievance against the Slash Y and where they intended hiding out between raids. It was a lot of maybes, Simpson had to admit, but there was only one way to find out if the maybes became facts.

'We'll do that, Pete,' he said. 'Pay them another visit.' Then, raising his voice, he called out, 'Let's move out, boys!'

Drummond couldn't leave fast enough. Not only did he want to get within touching distance of the young girl again, he was worried that the sodbuster, on seeing his corn ground into the dust, could just maybe find his balls and poke his rifle through the window of the shack and cut loose at them. Drummond eased his horse between two of his men to make sure that any shot wouldn't end up in his back.

Carla, busy in the kitchen, heard the sound of a fast-moving rider closing in on the *hacienda*. A few minutes later her father came bursting into the kitchen. That and his alarmed look told her that the rider hadn't been the bearer of good news.

'Señor Castro's boy has just ridden in!' her father said. 'Simpson and his men have destroyed his father's standing corn and that they could be heading this way. Simpson is seeking information about Mr Larribee and young Blaze and he's prepared to raise hell in the valley to come by it!'

'But . . . but I thought that the two *señors* were in Arizona,' Carla stammered.

'So did I,' replied Brewster. 'Though it don't seem so. But I have to think of your safety so pack up a few clothes as quick as you can. Your aunt is helping Tomas to hitch up the mule to the buggy. He's going to take you to La Paz, just across the Mexican border, where you can stay with kin of Aunt Sofia's. I'm staying with the peons to defend the *hacienda*. When Simpson stops his rampaging I'll send word for you to come back.'

'But I want to stay with you, Father!' Carla cried. 'I can use a gun!'

'You do as I say, girl!' Brewster said, in a harshness of voice Carla hadn't heard him use to her before. 'A boy had to kill a man on your behalf and brought this trouble on to the Mexican farmers! And do you want Pete Drummond to force himself on to you again?'

Carla recoiled as though her father had struck her a blow with his fist. She thought of Señor Blaze, a boy she had a fond likeness for, here in New Mexico, risking being shot by the *compadres* of the pig who had tried to deflower her. She began to sob.

Brewster wanted to put his arms round his daughter to comfort her. She hadn't been responsible for Bull Drummond's death, the horn dog son-of-a-bitch had brought it on himself but he wanted Carla to leave the *hacienda*, be out of reach of Pete Drummond's dirty paws, even if it meant lying to her.

A quietly sobbing Carla hurried into her room and began blindly throwing a change of clothes into a carpet bag. Ten minutes later she was sitting alongside Tomas, an elderly peon, in the buggy, still damp cheeked. Tomas cracked the whip above the mule's ears and the buggy rolled forward. Glancing over her shoulder, Carla saw her father holding a rifle, standing more straight-backed now, on the front porch with the rest of the *hacienda*'s peons. Then the trail dipped and the place was lost from her sight and she was left with her worrying, sickening thoughts of the fearful danger her father and the peons were facing and the feeling she was running out on them. She dared not think about the possible fate of Señor Blaze and his *compadre*, Señor Larribee.

★ ★ ★

The Slash Y revenge seekers halted their mounts in a slight flurry of hoof-raised dust on a rise overlooking the *hacienda* close enough to see that their riding in was expected. Simpson cursed. He had come here to put pressure on folk to loosen up their tongues, not to partake in a gunfight. If he made an aggressive move, the five rifle-armed men standing on the *hacienda* porch would gun them down.

'That greaser kid musta warned them that we could be payin' them a visit,' Drummond growled.

Simpson didn't answer him. Whoever had warned the owner of the *hacienda* didn't matter. What mattered was that he would get no answers to his questions here. He'd been outwitted.

For several minutes he jaundiced-eyed the *hacienda* then a sudden movement caught his attention as one of his crew drew away from the line of riders and cut across the open, well to the left of the house.

'Where the hell is Sancho going,

Drummond?' he grated.

'I dunno, boss,' replied an equally puzzled Drummond. 'Hang on though, there's a bunch of woollies comin' outa that dip so I figure Sancho has gone to have words with his cousin.' He gave a thin grin. 'M'be he's goin' to ask his cousin to stampede his sheep, Texas style, in the direction of the *hacienda* allowin' us to fireball in behind the dust cloud they'll raise.'

Simpson, in no mood for humour, gave him a hard-eyed glare, then gave the order to pull back off the ridge to wait for the return of Sancho. Knowing that if they didn't hit the next farm soon the Mexican boy would have alerted the whole valley of their intentions and they could be running headlong into big trouble, men willing to make a stand against them. Then their only edge, riding in on Mexican families when they were isolated, would be gone. Simpson was mad enough to shoot Sancho out of his saddle if he couldn't put forward a good reason for wasting time they couldn't afford to lose by wanting to talk to his kinsman.

It was a scowling, impatient Simpson who eyeballed Sancho on his return. Before he could rant at him for holding back the operation Sancho said, 'I thought you'd like to know how many guns we were facin' boss, if you were decidin' to make a fight of it, so I rode across to see my cousin when I saw him bringin' in his sheep. He told me that all the men who work the land on the *hacienda* are on the porch. Except one old peon drivin' a buggy with a young girl in it who was headin' south on the Mexican trail not ten minutes or so ago.'

It was an equally impatient Drummond, eager to feel again the firm warm flesh of the girl, who saw the chance to win back the advantage they had lost.

'That buggy won't have much of a head start, boss, on me and Sancho pushin' our horses hard along that old Comanche war trail.' We'll be able to stop it rollin' a long ways before it reaches the border. He smiled for real. 'Then you'll have that sutler more willin' to pour out his heart.'

Simpson did some rapid thinking. Drummond was right: the girl as a hostage gave him the winning hand.

'Right, get going!' he snapped. 'But no fooling around with the girl, *comprende*?' His fierce-eyed look wiped the smile off his straw boss's face. 'We've wasted enough time as it is. We'll wait for you at the creek.'

'OK, Sancho, let's ride!' Drummond said, and jabbed his heels into his horse's flanks. Simpson's order had put him in a black dog mood though he consoled himself with the licentious thought that the longer he had to wait to get his way with the girl the greater pleasure it would give him when that time came. And by hell, he told himself, that day would come or his name wasn't Pete Drummond.

★ ★ ★

Tomas's nerves twanged as he heard the grating noise on the nearside wheel become dangerously louder. He had kept the mule reined in hoping that at a slow speed the faulty wheel would hold fast. If the wheel came off there was no way he and the *señorita* could lift up the weighty buggy to slip the wheel back on. Even if he had a new pin to fix in the axle.

He had tried to tell Señorita Sofia, when she came into the barn and ordered him to hitch up the mule to the buggy as the Señorita Carla had to be driven to La Paz pronto, that without a new axle pin he was heating in the fire the buggy would hardly make it as far as the creek before the wheel came off.

'The old pin will have to do,' she had said. 'The *señorita* will be in great danger if she stays at the *hacienda*. The Slash Y *gringo* pigs are riding here.'

Tomas knew what had happened to Señorita Carla at the store at the hands of one of the cattlemen and the fearful beating her father had suffered. Without any more protesting he headed for the stable.

He didn't tell the *señorita* about the likelihood of a wheel slipping off, the girl had enough worries on her mind. Then what he feared happened: the loose wheel bounced over a large stone on the edge of the trail and the wheel wobbled on the last inch or so of axle, tilting the buggy over. A nerve jangling Carla shrieked in terror. Only Tomas's quick reactions in jerking the mule to a halt in its own length prevented the buggy from turning completely over on its side.

'It's OK, *señorita*,' he said. 'The wheel's still on. I'll soon tighten it up,' his smile hid his lie.

Tomas pushed back his drooping-brimmed sombrero and scratched his head as he looked at the loose wheel. Though it was still on the axle the buggy would have to be lifted bodily several inches to push it firmly back on to the axle. A task maybe he and the *señorita* could manage. But how would the wheel stay on without a new pin?

Before he could come up with a solution, Carla's sudden cry of alarm had him facing another problem, a much more serious one — two riders coming into view, fast, from a narrow cut in a low ridge on the east of the trail. They were too far away for Tomas to recognize them but he had no doubts that they were Slash Y men who had used the old Indian trail to cut them off.

Not wanting to offend the *señorita* Tomas held back his curses. Señorita Sofia had entrusted him to take the young *señorita* to safety and by the Holy *Madre*, or *El Diablo*, Tomas was desperate enough to accept help from either, he would honour the *señora*'s orders. Resolute-faced he picked up his rifle from the floor of the buggy then took hold of Carla's arm and led her down into a dry gully running behind the buggy. He favoured her with another one of his false smiles.

'You keep low, *señorita*, and you'll

come to no harm,' he told her and levered a shell into the chamber of the Winchester.

Carla was too numbed with fear to do anything but cover her head with her arms and press herself tight into the side of the gully.

Tomas took aim at the leading rider and pulled off a shot. It passed harmlessly over Drummond's head but had him pulling up his horse sharply and leaping out of his saddle, gripping his rifle as he flung himself flat on the ground. Sancho, also knowing that a rifleman, lying in a good firing position, had all the edge over two riders only able to use their pistols on the move, followed Drummond in eating dirt.

Tomas crouched low and laid a comforting arm across the trembling Carla's shoulders as shells from two rifles raised dirt spouts along the rim of the gully. The fusillade suddenly stopped and Tomas risked a quick look over the edge. He saw the two horses but he could see no signs of their riders.

Then he was forced to duck down once more as the firing started up again. This time only one rifle was firing, single, regular, pinning-down shots, a change of tactics by their pursuers that had Tomas realizing that one of the sons-of-bitches was trying to outflank him.

Soon the *señorita* would find out that telling her she would come no harm had been lies. And that hurt as much as the shells would when they came winging this way. In between firing at the rifleman ahead of him, he cast fearful glances along the gully. Twenty or so yards to his left, the gully turned sharply, a blind corner from where a man could back shoot him without risking his own life.

★ ★ ★

Fierro and Gomez, foot sore and thirsty, were just about to call off their futile search for the Slash Y crew and return to camp when they heard the sound of gunfire in the direction of the main trail. They looked hopefully at each other; maybe their scouting wasn't going to be a waste of time after all. No longer feeling tired, they set off in long, loping, ground-eating strides to the sound of the firing.

Tomas had never sweated so much doing nothing in his life before. Above the noise of the gunfire he tried to listen for the rattle of loose stones, which, he thought forebodingly, would be the last sound he heard, other than the shot that would kill him. Then he would go to Heaven, or Hell, cursed until Judgement Day for failing to protect the young *señorita*.

When Tomas heard the blood-chilling rattling Doomsday noise it came not from where he had been watching but from along the gully to his right. He whirled round, panicky-eyed, finger fumbling frantically for the rifle's trigger, and found himself gazing at two Mexican boys. They may be only *chicos* but they were armed, and that made it

186

three rifles against two. And grasping at straws, Tomas could see the possibility of safely delivering the *señorita* to her kin in Mexico. As his unexpected help came nearer he saw that both boys had the watchful-eyed faces of the border *hombre*, and knew that he was looking at two of Pablo Villa's grandsons, boys who had been hunted by Simpson and his men for their daring raids against his herds. Tomas had no doubts now that he would be able carry out Señora Sofia's wishes.

★　★　★

The brothers had seen the abandoned buggy on the trail and saw the muzzle flashes of a rifle on the ridge opposite them firing on someone sheltering in a gully close by the buggy. Their excitement cooled down, their sweat-raising dash had been for nothing. It seemed that they had stumbled on a shoot-out between a *bandido*, whose ambush plans had gone wrong, and whoever was driving the buggy. It was no business of theirs, they weren't *gringo* lawmen.

Fierro nudged Gomez. 'Watch to the left of that clump of bush,' he said.

A puzzled-eyed Gomez did as he was told and fixed his gaze on the brush. In a few moments a tall, thickset *gringo* came out into the open, to drop down quickly out of sight into an arroyo leading to the gully and the man pinned down in it by the rifle fire from the high ground. Gomez drew in his breath with a loud hiss.

'Did you get a good look at that *gringo*, Gomez?' he heard his brother ask.

Gomez turned and faced his brother. '*Sí*, he is a Slash Y dog,' he replied flat-voiced. 'We have seen him many times guarding the herds we were trying to take cattle from. It is our fight now, Fierro. We must go to to the aid of that *hombre* from the buggy before that dog kills him!'

The pair set off running again,

188

dropping down into an arroyo to shield them from the other Slash Y rifleman.

To the brothers' surprise not only was there an *hombre*, an elderly, anxious-faced Mexican in the gully, but they also saw the huddled figure of a young *señorita*. Gomez had been doubly right, Fierro thought, in saying that it was now their fight.

* * *

'Simpson and his men are raiding the Mexican farms in the valley!' Tomas burst out. 'They're seeking information about two *gringo pistoleros*!' Tomas didn't see the quick look that passed between the brothers as both of them thought with some pride that they, not Señor Blaze and Felix, had discovered the whereabouts of the Slash Y riders.

'The *señorita*'s name is Carla Brewster,' Tomas said. 'Her father owned the sutler's store but it was burnt down on Simpson's orders and one of his men injured him badly.' Not wanting to

189

embarrass Carla, Tomas did not mention that she was almost raped. 'So he thought it safer for Carla to stay with kinfolk in Mexico until the Slash Y dogs rode out of the valley. I was taking her there when one of the buggy's wheels came loose and slowed us down.' Tomas spat angrily. 'Allowing two of the Slash Y men to catch up with us! One of them is firing at us from across the trail, his *compadre* must be closing in on this gully.'

'We know where the dog is, *señor*,' Fierro replied. Standing proud he smiled down at Carla. 'You will come to no harm, *señorita*,' he said. 'You have my and my brother, Gomez's, word.'

Carla straightened up and favoured him with a ghost of a thankful smile.

Then Fierro, being the older brother, by one year, gave out the orders. Curt-voiced he said, 'You, *señor*, keep firing back at that *hombre*, you stay here, Gomez, but don't use your rifle. We want to keep that *hombre* we saw still thinking that there is only one gun here.' His face hardened. 'If I fail to kill the dog, then it will be up to you to honour our promise to the *señorita*.'

Before Gomez could say otherwise, Fierro was trotting along the gully, rifle held high across his chest. Gomez put on a bold *pistolero*'s face for the *señorita* and the old *señor*'s sake, and began to keen-eye the bend in the gully where the *hombre* he had to kill would show up if things had gone badly for his brother.

Drummond paused for a breather. The arroyo was a sun trap making it hotter than hell for him. He grinned, but the prize would be worth all the sweat he was raising. He listened for a moment or two to the sound of the regular rifle fire; Sancho was playing his part in keeping the old greaser fully occupied until he was close enough in to back shoot him. Simpson had warned him that he hadn't to mess about with the girl, but when he grabbed hold of her to bundle her back to the horses there would be plenty of time to put his hands where he craved them to be. That thought stretched his grin into a genuine smile.

His smile was still there when a Mexican boy suddenly appeared in front of him. Fierro had never killed a man before but his hatred for the men who had killed his mother and father wouldn't prevent him from doing so now. In a sweeping movement he swung his rifle outwards and from point-blank range fired two shots.

Drummond only had time to change his smile into a wide-eyed look of shock and horror before the two shells crushed in his chest and he choked on his own blood as he stumbled back several paces, rifle falling from his grasp.

With his rifle now held in trembling hands, Fierro watched the *gringo* collapse to the ground and waited until his final dying limb-twitching ended, then turned to make it back to the gully.

Gomez, on hearing the two shots

wanted to run to find out who had fired them — Fierro or the *gringo* — but forced himself to hold his ground. Though he didn't like to consider it, he could be dashing wildly over the dead body of Fierro and into the *gringo* rifle fire, then who would look out for the *señorita*? Behind him he heard Carla sobbing quietly. He dared not face the old *señor*, not wanting to show him the fear he was feeling.

Sancho was doing his own share of worrying. The shots he had heard came from nowhere near the old man who was still firing at him. A cold chill swept over him as he got the frightening feeling that Pete could have run into the *hombres* they were seeking. Were the boss and the rest of the crew looking in the wrong part of the range for the two *gringo pistoleros*?

'Are you OK, Pete?' he called out. On hearing no reply he began to think rapidly of number one, the saving of his own skin, and to hell with Simpson's orders to bring the girl back. Eyes popping, Sancho cast wide searching glances below him, trying to spot any patch of brush shaking or hearing the crack of a dead branch being stepped on, warning him that the *pistoleros* were coming for him. Slowly he kneed and elbowed his way back to the horses.

Gomez heard the bird call and broke into a wide smile. 'The *gringo* dog is dead!' he cried. 'That bird call is from Fierro to let me know that he is OK!'

To prove his words Fierro came into view, stone-faced as though gunning down *mal hombres* was an every day chore. Gomez rushed to embrace him but Fierro held up a restraing hand.

'Our task is not finished yet,' he said. 'That rifleman on the ridge can still prevent us from getting to the buggy.'

Tomas lowered his rifle and turned and grinned at them. 'The way is clear, *amigos*, I've just seen two horses being led over the rimline, but the Slash Y dog was too low down for me to get a shot at him.'

Fierro and Gomez were all smiles as

they congratulated each other. Carla, who was up on her feet, was less taut-nerved enough to care about her appearance, and began brushing the dust from her dress and finger combing her long black hair.

Tomas, his worried look back on his face, said, 'This is as far as the buggy will go; the *señorita* could ride on the mule, but more Slash Y *hombres* could come along the old trail and a horse would soon catch up with a mule. I could try and hold them back with my rifle, but' — Tomas shrugged — 'on an open trail that would not be for long. The *señorita* would never reach Mexico.'

'Do not worry, *señor*,' Feirro said. 'We will take you to our camp, our *gringo compadres* have horses.' He smiled at Carla. 'They will make sure that you reach Mexico safely. Now you go and unhitch the mule, *señor*. You go with them, Gomez, and keep your rifle sighted on the ridge trail. I'll join you as soon as I pick up that dead *gringo*'s guns.'

They set off along the trail south, with Tomas at the head rope-leading the mule, seating Carla and her belongings, the brothers, grim-faced, bringing up the rear several yards behind them, practically walking sideways as they kept keen-eyed looks on their back trail. Not until Fierro gave Tomas the order to cut away from the trail and make for the high bluffs did he and Gomez relax their vigilance somewhat and take over the lead.

12

'Where the hell can the bastard be, Blaze?' Larribee said. 'Him and his crew ain't pleasure ridin' around the territory. Simpson's makin' a move against us that's for sure. But what it is has me beat!'

Blaze had just finished telling Larribee how he and Felix had found the ranch only manned by a skeleton crew. He shrugged. 'Me, too, pard. All I know is that Simpson has one man less on his payroll. Felix here had to kill one of them.' He cold-grinned. 'And as good a kill as I've ever witnessed. It was only his quick thinkin' and slick work with his big knife I'm standin' here talkin' to you.'

By Larribee's slack-jawed look, Blaze knew what was passing through his partner's mind.

'Now don't start preachin' that

hogwash about death shadows again,' he said angrily. 'Felix had no choice. We were goin' into an armed enemy camp; it was odds on that we'd have to shed blood. If Felix hadn't done what he did it would have been our blood bein' spilt.'

Larribee closed his mouth and remained silent. The boys had made a trip into a Daniel's den, maybe with only a few of the lions in there, and they had done well to make it back here unharmed. But in spite of Blaze telling him that he ought not to fret about things that hadn't yet happened, he was worrying himself white-headed wondering what Simpson's moves against them were.

'You did OK, *compadres*,' he said. 'Especially you, Felix.' He didn't want to dampen the look of pride in Felix's eyes by saying he could be called upon to make several more *good* killings.

'Where are Fierro and Gomez, Señor Larribee?' Felix asked, a mite disappointed that his brothers weren't around to greet him and Señor Blaze. He was eager to tell them of the *good* killing that the *pistolero*, Señor Blaze, had praised him for.

'Like you and Blaze,' replied Larribee. 'They were itchin' to find out where the Slash Y crew are so they went out scoutin' along the northern rim of Simpson's land.' Larribee grinned. 'They were hopin' to get a jump on you boys by findin' out where those bastards are.' Larribee's face hardened. 'And like you two did, they've got me worried.'

Villa, who was standing the watch on a rocky outcrop, shouted that the boys were coming in but accompanied by two men, one of them a rider, and had the three swinging up their rifles and scattering for cover.

Fierro's faint-sounding cry of, 'We're bringing in two *amigos*, Señor Larribee!' rapidly eased their taut, last stand nerves and they got to their feet wondering who the *amigos* were.

Blaze let out a laugh. 'Why that rider

ain't an *hombre*, Villa!' he cried. 'It's Señorita Brewster!' He was getting his wish of seeing the sweet-smiling girl again sooner than he expected. Though the state he was in, after scrambling along dry washes and through patches of brush, he sure wouldn't cut a favourable impression with her. Then, thinking realistically it wouldn't matter if he was dressed up as smart as some Dapper Dan, her knowing that he was a man who hired out his gun, a *pistolero*, she, a finely raised *señorita*, would hardly give him the time of day. And besides, right now he was in the middle of a shooting war. Trying to spark up to a girl would have his ever-fretting partner casting him a fish-eyed look. Though looking like a saddle-bum didn't stop him from dashing forward to help Señorita Carla dismount from the mule. Carla rewarded him with a shy smile and a murmured, '*Gracias*, Señor Blaze.' The Señor Blaze broad-grinned and renewed his earlier pledge that he would shoot down any Slash Y son-of-a-bitch who attempted to lay his hands on her. Then Fierro and Gomez began to talk rapidly in their own language about their adventures to Felix.

'OK, boys, let's have it one at a time and in plain Yankee!' Larribee snapped. 'But first, you get up there with old Villa, Blaze; your eyes are keener than his! We don't want to be surprised out here in the open by the fellas we can't find!' Not when the girl, he and Blaze had been killing and winging men to protect, would be in danger again. They would have been risking their lives for damn all, he thought.

He turned and faced the boys once more. 'Ain't you goin' to introduce me to your *amigo*, Fierro?' he asked mock gruffly. 'Or didn't your grandpappy teach you any manners?'

'Oh, *sí*, yes, Señor Larribee!' a flushed-faced Fierro stammered. 'He is Señor Tomas who tends Señora Sofia's horses at her *hacienda*. He was taking Señorita Carla to Mexico out of reach

201

of the Slash Y dogs. They are raiding the Mexican farms looking for you. Two of them caught up with the *señor* when his buggy wheel came loose.' Fierro stiffened up with pride and in a matter-of-fact voice said, 'And I killed one of them; his *compadre* thought it wise not to face our guns, Señor Larribee, and rode away. I brought them here hoping that they could use your horses to get them to Mexico. Did I do right, *compadre*?'

'Yeah, you did the right thing, Fierro,' replied Larribee, taken aback somewhat by the boy's bare statement that he'd killed a Slash Y man. He had sold the brothers short; they were proving that they could stand as equals alongside him and Blaze. He didn't need Mr William Bonney and his Boys, he had raised a gang of his own.

'A boy whose father's corn had been trampled down by the Slash Y men,' Tomas broke in, 'rode to the *hacienda* to warn Señor Brewster that the *gringo* dog, Simpson was coming to question him again about the two *gringo pistoleros* who were shooting his men. Señora Sofia ordered me to take Señorita Carla to her kin in La Paz where she would be safe until Simpson returned to his ranch. Then it was as the young *hombre* said. Two Slash Y men caught up with me as I was trying to fix the buggy's loose wheel. Fierro and Gomez saved my life and prevented those dogs from taking the *señorita* back to Simpson.'

Larribee looked back at the brothers again. 'I take it, Fierro, that Felix has already told you that he's also put paid to a Slash Y man. I reckon that the three of you ain't no longer *chicos* but full blown *hombres*.' He smiled. 'I'm sure glad you ain't gunnin' for me and Blaze.'

The three *hombres* grinned proudly at each other. Gomez silently promising himself that he would draw some Slash Y's blood soon.

Larribee then got to the business that had brought Tomas and the girl here.

'Fierro, Gomez,' he said. 'I'd be obliged if you'd go and saddle up the horses and bring them out here, quick like. Felix, you take over the watch from Blaze.'

An intrigued Blaze clambered down from the lookout rock and joined Larribee and the camp's unexpected visitors, one more than welcome. Larribee introduced him to the old Mexican before telling him that he would like him to act as escort to the pair to see that they made it to Mexico without any trouble.

'Simpson and his crew are raisin' hell north of here, Blaze,' he continued. 'The señora who the señorita and her pa were stayin' with thought it wise to send her to relatives in Mexico out of harm's way. Señor Tomas was given the job of gettin' her there but Simpson sent two of his men after the buggy and caught up with it. Only the showin' up of Fierro and Gomez prevented the señor bein' killed and the girl captured. I figure that Simpson wants to use the *señorita* as a hostage to force her pa to tell all he knows about us. Fierro, usin' his brains, brought them here for them to borrow our horses. They'd never make it to Mexico with Tomas on foot. And just for the record, Fierro shot dead one of the Slash Y men and scared off the other.' Before Blaze got over his surprise at Fierro's actions, he said, 'The boys are seein' to the horses.'

Larribee could see by the gleam in Blaze's eyes that he would run barefooted alongside the *señorita*'s horse all the way to Mexico and willingly shoot any man, critter, or whatever who tried to stop him from getting the girl to safety.

'OK, *compadre*,' Blaze said, trying not to do a jig and holler out at his stroke of good luck to ride with the *señorita*.

'But that means you will be one man short if Simpson and his men attack you, Señor Larribee,' Carla said, surprising both men. 'I am sure that Señor Tomas will stay here and take

Señor Blaze's place. Maybe Simpson will send more of his men to take me, and a slow riding mule would hold the horses back.' Carla smiled at Larribee and he got a touch of the good feeling Blaze must be enjoying.

'Yeah, that makes sense, señorita,' he said. 'You'll have to move fast; the whole of Simpson's crew could come by this way soon. Señor Tomas is welcome to stay, but it's his choice if he wants to take part in our fight.'

'I've already taken part in your fight, Señor Larribee,' Tomas said. 'Back there at the buggy.' His leathery face cracked in a wide smile. 'And I'd willingly face Simpson and all of his scum rather than ride that bony-backed mule all the way to La Paz without a saddle.'

Larribee thought that in spite of the old man's keenness to join them he wouldn't be as expert with a gun as Blaze was. Then realizing he could be underestimating Tomas's capabilities, as he had done with the brothers, he said, and meant it, 'Now we ain't a gun short, *señorita*.'

Carla surprised them again by asking for a rifle. 'You and Señor Blaze and the boys and Tomas have risked your lives to protect me. Am I not entitled to protect myself, Señor Larribee?'

Larribee looked her full in the eyes and meeting her steady, determined-eyed gaze, said, 'That you are, *señorita*, that you are. I'll see that there's a long gun in the saddle boot.'

★ ★ ★

Blaze and Carla were ready to move out. Blaze, bold-eyed, had his rifle resting across the saddle horn, a shell in its chamber, ready for split second action.

'I don't know how far it is to La Paz, Blaze,' Larribee said. 'But I reckon you'll not make it in daylight, so don't attempt to ride back here in the dark. Simpson and his men are lookin' for us in real earnest and they could be hangin' around close by. If you happen to bump into them you'll be handicapped by rope-leadin' my horse.' He grinned. 'The *señorita*'s friends are sure to have a rat-free barn where a *gringo* can snatch a coupla hours' sleep.' He lightly slapped the rump of Blaze's horse. 'OK, *amigo*, off you go, and ride fast.' And shoot true if you have to pull out your guns, he added under his breath.

As Blaze pulled away he called over his shoulder, 'Don't you young *pistoleros* shoot down all those Slash Y men; leave one or two for me to dispatch!'

Larribee watched the pair ride out, the *señorita* sitting astride her mount like a man, and hoped to hell that the death shadow wasn't riding alongside them. Blaze wouldn't want his killing streak to show in front of the girl he was trying to impress. He turned and caught a glimpse of Tomas's worried look.

'Your charge is in safe hands, *amigo*,' he said. 'That boy once raised hell with

Billy the Kid up Fort Sumner way. It will have to be one sharp *hombre* to catch him unawares. Come, Tomas, I reckon you'll not say no to a mug of coffee.' Raising his voice he said, 'One of you boys take the *señor*'s mule in and see that it's fed and watered. The other two take over your grandfather's watch. Anything you see that gets you worried come in fast and let me know.'

★ ★ ★

Carla smiled to herself. She was riding, on her own, with a *gringo*. Her Aunt Sofia wouldn't even allow her to sit on the *hacienda* porch with a Mexican boy she knew unless she was sitting between them. Her father had told her that Señor Blaze and his elderly *compadre* were *gringo pistoleros, mal hombres*, yet by his action, killing the man who would have deflowered her, Señor Blaze had proved himself a true *caballero*, a gentleman — she smiled again — though not a finely dressed one.

Carla shot a sidelong glance at her *caballero*, noting the bold lines of his face as he kept looking over his shoulder for any signs of danger to them. Yet not since that fearful day had she felt so at peace with herself. She was curious to know more about him. Was he staying in New Mexico when this terrible trouble ended, and how he came by that streak of white in his hair when he couldn't be that much older than she was. Then Carla gasped. She hadn't even thanked him for coming to her aid! What must he be thinking of her? Ungrateful, too proud a Mexican *señorita* to thank a *gringo bandido* for risking his life on her behalf?

'Señor Blaze,' she said hesitantly. 'I hope you will forgive me for not thanking you for coming to my aid at the store — '

'No apology needed, *señorita*,' a wide smiling Blaze interrupted. 'What with that sonuva — that fella roughin' you about, then the buggy bein' ambushed, your mind's been otherwise occupied.

You're here with me now, that's the best thanks,' he added boldly. He wasn't sure but he thought that she had blushed and judged that he had said enough, though he had strong feelings for her. Most of the talking he'd had with females was the bawdy and lewd bantering that he and Billy and the rest of the boys had exchanged with the short-time girls in the cat-houses and saloons, language not fit for a well-bred *señorita* to hear. He hoped that she would think his tongue-tiedness was because his attention was fixed on their back trail and the trouble that could come pounding along it.

Carla's saying that her uncle's house was not far away eased his embarrassment.

On coming up to the house, a large two-storeyed adobe and timber-built building, well served by barns, Blaze realized that Carla's uncle was the big *hombre* in this part of Mexico and he had no doubts that if he had not been in the company of his niece he, a *gringo*

211

drifter, would have been ordered off the *hacienda* with guns pointed at him to speed him on his way.

As Carla dismounted outside the house, a tall grey-haired man stepped out on to the porch. His face broke into a surprised but welcoming smile on seeing Carla and stepped forward and embraced her. Though Blaze saw the old man giving him a piercing-eyed look.

Carla slipped out of his arms and began to talk rapidly to him in Mexican. Blaze shuffled uneasily in his saddle. The old man heard her out and once more looked at Blaze, with disbelief at first, then his smile returned.

'Step down, Señor Blaze,' he said in English, 'and accept the hospitality of my house. Carla has told me of her father's trouble with the *gringo* rancher, Simpson, and how you killed a man to save her honour. And that you have ridden here with her to protect her from further harm.'

'*Muchas gracias, señor,*' replied Blaze.

Before he could swing down from his saddle, four girls about Carla's age, came rushing out of the house smiling and giggling with delight and crowded round their cousin. And Blaze heard more rapid-fire Mexican and the four girls gazed at him with rounded eyes. Then came more giggling and their searching gazes passed between him and Carla. And Blaze sat tight. No way was he going to take up the old man's hospitality, not with four young females laughing behind his back at his ragged-assed appearance. When he was forced to take off his hat they would have fits.

'I thank you again, señor,' he said. 'But I must ride back to my *compadres* pronto to tell them that the *señorita* is in safe hands. Though I'd be obliged if I could water the horses before I ride out.' He evaded Carla's looks hoping she would understand the reason for his lie.

'As you wish, señor,' Carla's uncle replied. He shouted out a name and a peon came running round the corner of

213

the house. 'Show the *señor* where the water tanks are, Pedro!'

As Blaze watered the horses he thought of disobeying Larribee's order and riding back to the camp in the dark to put as much distance between him and Carla, fast, then decided against it. His partner may be a worrier but it had kept him alive a long time, for a bank robber. It could make life-saving sense to do as he had advised him.

He spun round on hearing Carla who had come up behind, say, 'Must you go, Señor Blaze?'

He grinned at her embarrassedly. 'You can see I ain't dressed for social visitin', *señorita*,' he replied. 'I'd be outa place here with five pretty *señoritas* hangin' around me. But that don't mean I ain't disappointed at not bein' able to take up your uncle's kindly invite,' he added hastily.

'I don't think we shall see each other again,' Carla said, trembling-voiced. 'My uncle wants my father and me to come and live here in Mexico so the *gringo* dogs won't try and molest me again.' She smiled wanly. 'His words not mine.' Then, ignoring her strict social upbringing, and feeling a warm-blooded urge to do so, she reached forward and kissed her *gringo caballero* full on the lips. With a sobbed, 'Go with God, Blaze!' she turned and ran back to the house. Leaving Blaze smiling a moon-faced surprised grin.

Blaze had had good times in his wild life before but none tasting as sweet, and yet as bitter. But that was the way it had to be. No Mexican father would think that a penniless *gringo* gunman was worthy of his daughter's friendship.

As he rode out, Blaze thought it ill-mannered of him not to to thank Carla's uncle again, but the break between him and Carla had been made and that was best for both of them. And what the hell, he thought, cold, hungry camps were a regular pastime to him.

13

The lamps in the big house stayed lit well into the early hours as Simpson, sitting at his desk chewing away at the end of a long dead cigar, thought through his present dilemma.

Building up his spread had brought him the good days of seeing his herd grow, and the bad days of holding on to his grand dream by beating off Mexican *bandidos*, bronco Comanche thieves and *gringo* cattle lifters. But none of them had him so low in mood and frustrated anger as the brand of killer misfits he was facing now. Two border drifters and three ragged-assed Mexican kids were picking off his crew whenever they had the opportunity to catch his men unawares, and it seemed that he could do damn all to stop them. Simpson spat out the shredded stump of his cigar to do some

216

loud-voiced cursing.

Riding back to the Slash Y from the valley, burdened with the grim fact that he had lost another straw boss, then a hand meeting them on the trail with the shock news that the bastards came close enough to the well-guarded ranch practically to decapitate a man with a machete, made yesterday one hell of a bad day for him.

His crew were a bunch of hard *hombres*, some of them having wanted notices posted on them before they signed up to tend his cows, but, as they rode the rest of the way to the ranch, there was none of the usual joshing backchat passing between them. He could sense their uneasiness. All, including him, had been casting all-seeing glances across the plain. From any of the gullies and arroyos that criss-crossed it a rifle shot could suddenly ring out and empty another saddle. To try to run down the drygulcher on horseback could put them in the back sights of another ambusher. They may be border riffraff and three Mex kids but they fought like the eastern forest Indians once did, on foot, and he had to admit begrudgingly that the sons-of-bitches were doing it well.

Simpson took out another cigar from the box on his desk and put a match to it then sat back in his chair and began to think like a man who had carved a cattle empire out of an untamed land.

One thing was for sure, he reasoned, if the raiders moved around on foot they'd be holed up close to where they had done their killing and wounding, somewhere on his own range. His trip into the Mexican farmland had been a waste of time, he thought bitterly, and had got him a man killed. Though the farmer whose corn he'd had destroyed had mentioned that the Mexican boys were camped out in the Black Ridge buttes, and the two *gringo* shootists could be with them.

It was a wild shot hunting for them among the buttes but no wilder than hard-assing all over the territory trying to pin them down. Simpson gave a bared-toothed grin. This time his boys would go Indian as well so that they would raise no give away trail dust. The cigar end glowed red as he drew on it in a more settled state of mind.

14

It was a cold Blaze, half asleep, still thinking of Carla, who heard the grunting and snorting of the longhorns from a draw to the left of the trail. He had heard them moving around on the way south with Carla, but now he pulled off the trail and rode across to have a closer look at the cows. The draw reached well back into the hills and he could see that it was a sizeable herd fattening themselves on the ripe grass. And it was as he had thought, the cows were part of Simpson's herd he and the boys had spooked. It also meant that he was close to, or on, Slash Y land. When Blaze rode back to the trail all the wishful maybes and hopes regarding him and Señorita Carla were put aside. If he didn't stay alert he would have no future to harbour pleasant thoughts about the girl.

An hour or so after he had seen the cows, Blaze saw the purple smudge of the rocky bluffs on the horizon. He was definitely riding across Simpson's range and he gripped his rifle tighter. Then, out of the corner of his eye, he caught a sudden flash of light. It could have been a shaft of sunlight reflecting off a seam of quartz in a boulder, or bouncing off a rifle barrel. Blaze gave a grimace of a grin. It wasn't only his partner who was a worrier.

He saw more sun glints ahead of him covering a wide front and quickly realized that he had every right to be worried. Simpson, the son-of-a-bitch, was out there with his men, using the same Indian tactics as they were. He dismounted sharply and led both horses off the trail and on to the lower ground and pressed forward on foot with some speed to warn Larribee of the new danger. That's if he could swing wide of Simpson's line of skirmishers.

Larribee, on first daylight watch, thinking of how Blaze was making out with the *señorita* and that he'd probably spent the night in a real bed and eaten well before lying down his head, jerked up in surprise as his young partner popped into view from an arroyo, rein-leading both horses. It seemed that Blaze had had the bad luck of both horses going lame on him. He was about to learn that lame horses were the least of his problems.

'We've got trouble, Mr Larribee!' a dust and sweat-streaked Blaze called out as he stopped beneath the lookout post. 'Simpson and his crew ain't more than three or four miles behind me, movin' this way on foot! I spotted six of them but the rest are out there somewhere. I had to go real wide to make certain I'd got clear of them.'

'So the bastard has learned from us!' Larribee said, face twisted in anger. 'My grand plan of havin' his boys chasin' their own butts all over the range allowin' us to come and go as we please ain't goin' to work no more. But good work spottin' them, Blaze. It's givin' me time to come up with another grand plan.' He remained silent for a moment or two as he looked across the flat praying that Simpson's men were as far away as Blaze opined. If the bastards suddenly appeared in front of him and Blaze they were dead men. 'When you get to the camp ask one of the boys to come out and take over my watch.' Larribee gave a ghost of a smile. 'It's time for what the army generals call a council of war, Blaze.'

When Gomez clambered up on to the rock to relieve him, Larribee told him of the grim news Blaze had brought in. 'So keep a good watch, *amigo*, and keep outa sight, OK?'

'That's good, *señor*, that Simpson and his dogs are close by,' Gomez said. 'Then I'll be able to kill one as my brothers have.'

Larribee favoured Gomez with a long thoughtful look before leaving. The brothers were beginning to disturb him. He was seeing another three Blazes' with their death shadows in the making.

Villa and Tomas were sitting at the fire when Larribee came into the camp. Blaze was standing behind him spooning down a can of cold beans which made him think that the kid hadn't eaten well down there in Mexico and by his drawn *hombre*'s features, it seemed that he hadn't slept well either. He called out for Felix and Fierro, who were watering the horses, to come and join them.

'Your grandsons are entitled to sit in on this palaver, Señor Villa,' he said. 'They've proved themselves *hombres*.'

He sat down at the fire and poured himself out a mug of coffee, sipping at it as his mind chewed over their options, his small army eagerly waiting for his new orders.

'I reckon you all know about Simpson workin' his way towards these bluffs,' he began. 'He knows we must be holed-up here and he's hopin' that his men, prowlin' around on foot and keepin' low, will catch us in their rifle sights the next time we go out and burn

224

down one of his line cabins or whatever. Whether or not we like it, *amigos*, we've lost our only edge. The bastard is takin' the fight to us, with more men.'

'We don't need to fight them on their terms, Señor Larribee,' Villa said. 'Even if Simpson knows our camp is in the Black Ridge buttes it will take him weeks to find it, then we won't be here. And he can't keep his men out in the sun, on foot, for many days. And we have food here and no shortage of water so we can stay here until he is forced to take his men back to the ranch.'

'Yeah, that's true, Señor Villa,' replied Larribee. 'We're better fixed to play the waitin' game. But Simpson means business, killin' business. He's stakin' everything on a shootout, to get rid of us once and for all. He'll not pull all his men back, m'be leave three, four men to keep an eye on these bluffs. When we do have to leave for supplies we'll risk walkin' in front of a Slash Y rifle. Now that, *amigos*, is too worrying a situation for yours truly. I favour takin' up Simpson's challenge and have one end-it-all shootout, though, bein' that I've picked out the spot for the gunfight, the odds will be in our favour, if I can rely on all of you bein' with me.' Larribee thin-smiled. 'Though not bein' an army general my plan, like my first one, could go all haywire and we could all end up dead.' He took a sip at his coffee while he waited for his *compadres*' reactions to his plea.

Fierro surprised him by speaking first. 'I say that we should hear Señor Larribee's plan, grandfather. And I know that I speak for Gomez and Felix also. It is a more honourable death to die fighting than be shot down from an ambush.' He looked apologetically at Larribee. 'That's if it is right for me to speak out, Señor Larribee.'

'It's OK, *compadre*,' replied Larribee. 'Every *hombre* at this camp has an equal say.' And you could get dead just as equally, he thought dourly.

Larribee saw old Villa's nod of

acceptance of his plan and the proud twist of his lips at his grandson's bold statement. Then he looked across at Tomas, the newcomer in the fight against Simpson. Before he could ask him if he was for or against his plan, Tomas spoke.

'Those two dogs who ambushed the buggy meant to kill me,' he said hard-voiced, 'and do worse to the *señorita*, so I am beholden to the young *hombres* for saving our lives. I will stand alongside them, Señor Larribee.'

'*Bueno, amigo*,' replied Larribee and turned his attention on to Blaze, a kid who had cut his teeth on gunfights. He was to play a leading, deadly role in carrying out his plan and when Blaze had had it explained to him he could figure that he wasn't about to risk his life on such a mad-assed scheme.

'Blaze', he said, 'no offence intended, but I'd like you to hold fire on your decision until you hear me out. Me and you are kinda goin' out on a limb.'

Blaze didn't need any plan, loco or

otherwise, to hit Simpson hard. He would raise the dust high riding right up to Simpson's fine house with his reins held between his teeth, firing away with two pistols if it meant that the threat against Carla was ended.

He grinned at Larribee. 'It's generally me who's placed you between a rock and a hard place; now it's your turn, you've got my vote.'

Larribee gave a relieved smile. He still had his small army. 'I'd be obliged if you'd pour me out a mug of coffee, Felix, then I'll explain where the killin' ground is and how we're goin' to get Simpson's boys strollin' across it.'

★ ★ ★

The Slash Y was out in full strength and Jack had drawn the short straw: he was standing the first watch. He was huddled down on a low brush-covered ridge carrying out Simpson's orders by searching every way and which way with the aid of a pair of field-glasses for signs of the men they were trying to track down. Jack cursed as the sweat running down his face distorted his vision. The other ten ranch hands were sitting in the shade below him. Simpson, sitting on his own, was having second thoughts about the wisdom of pulling most of his men off the ranch to seek out the raiders. He could be starting on a wild goose chase but he had a gut feeling he had done the right thing and a man had to follow his hunches. Jack's excited cry of, 'I see the sonsuvbitches, boss!' proved how right his inner feelings had been. He scrambled up on to the ridge, his crew at his heels.

'There boss, see 'em!' Jack said, pointing to his left. 'That's the kid who killed Bull and the tall fella with him was the bastard who crippled poor Billy!'

Simpson didn't need the offered glasses to see the two men, on foot, passing across their front, two men who were causing him a whole parcel of grief. He had the angry thought that they were returning from doing more harm to the Slash Y. '*Amigos*,' he muttered savagely, 'Your raiding days are about to end, in blood, your blood.'

'Why that's the scrawny kid who set about me and Saul!' Cal blurted out. 'Though that big fella weren't with him!' He brought up his rifle but before he could aim it Simpson knocked it down.

'Not yet, Cal, not yet!' he said. 'It seems, boys, that we're not facing a gang of raiders but two border gunmen and three greaser kids. Now we've got the chance to rope them all in.' He cold-grinned at Cal. 'You can have the same treat I promised Drummond to kind of make up for what he did to you. Now comes the tricky business. We've got to trail those two without them knowing or they'll spook and drop down into any one of the goddamned washes and we'll lose them. Being that we're not full-blood Comanches if we all start trailing them we'll alarm them

230

for sure, so, Cal, you and Lacey dog them, the rest of us will follow well behind.' He gave Cal a cold-eyed glare. 'Remember, it's not killing time yet. If you and Lacey tread lightly those two pilgrims ought to lead us right into their hole-up and the Mexican brats.'

15

Larribee and Blaze climbed out of the dry wash and into the open. They gave each other 'this is it' looks and set off walking the fair distance to the dark buttes, with the taut-legged gate of two hound dogs in heat. It was the testing time for Larribee's grand plan. The trap — Villa and his *compadres* the jaws, he and Blaze the bait — was set. Though the more Larribee ruminated over his grand scheme the more he began to think that the odds of its success weren't as great as he had stated. He tried to shrug away his doubts. After all this wasn't the first time he had put his life on the line, not for Blaze either and he could see no signs on his partner's face that he was having doubts about backing him up.

Larribee pointed ahead of him. 'That stretch of ground in front of that derelict hut, *amigos*, is the killin' ground that I spoke of.'

The site of the the proposed shoot-out had been chosen by Larribee after a quick scout of the range. Although the derelict building was roofless the crumbling adobe walls were still standing waist high in parts and would protect them from the Slash Y's return fire.

'And you reckon that when Simpson spots us he won't just have his boys gun us down, Mr Larribee?' Blaze asked.

'That's right, Blaze,' replied Larribee. 'I'm bankin' on Simpson wantin' to rope in our young *compadres* as well so if he spots us makin' for the buttes he'll take it that we're returnin' from a raid against his property and headin' for the hole-up he can't find. He'll rein in his men until he figures he's got us all in the bag. When the right moment comes, me and you, Blaze, will make a mad dash for that shack and draw the sonsuvbitches into the open.' He grinned at the jaws of his trap. 'We oughta clear those walls, *amigos*, before the Slash Y boys get over their surprise and start shootin'.'

'Then the *gringo* dogs will be facing seven rifles, not two,' Gomez said, eager to make his kill.

Larribee gave Gomez a flint-eyed look. 'But none of you fire until my say-so, we want them right into the trap before we spring it, OK? Unless me an Blaze get cut down before we reach the shack then it will be up to you, Señor Villa, to play it as you see it. My advice would be to cut and run for it back to the camp.'

'Many years before the cattlemen came this far south, Señor Larribee,' Villa said flat-voiced, 'this land was Mexican sheepherder land. When the cattle came they ate up the grass and drank the water holes dry, forcing the sheepherders to leave their land or starve.' Villa's face became as hard as his voice. That 'shack', *amigo*, was once a sheepherder's home, so it is a good place for sheepherders to kill

234

gringo cattlemen.'

The *compadres* wished each other good fortune then Larribee and Blaze began their long trek along the arroyas and gullies before swinging round to make the return trip in the open. The jaws of the trap settled down behind the shack's wall and checked over their rifles. If their *gringo compadres* did their task then they would not fail in playing their part.

★ ★ ★

Larribee, sweating with a mixture of the blazing heat and fear, stopped within sighting distance of their makeshift fort to relieve himself. 'Are the bastards behind us, Blaze?' he whispered hoarsely. 'It's right unsettling on the nerves, *amigo*, playin' the judas goat.'

'Your plan's workin', Mr Larribee,' Blaze replied. 'At least two of the bastards are workin' their way through that patch of brush we've just cleared.' Blaze grinned. 'They ain't makin a good job of trackin' us; they wouldn't fool a deaf Indian. Simpson will be keepin' the rest of his boys well back.' Blaze gave another grin. 'He don't want to alarm us bein' that we're leadin' him straight to our hole-up.'

'That's what I feared,' replied a gloomy-faced Larribee. 'I want the sonsuvbitches to come fireballin' across the killin' ground so that we can spring the trap. Those fellas back there will sit tight until Simpson and the rest of them come up then they'll tell him that we're bedded down in the old shack. Simpson, not wantin' to lose the edge he thinks he's he got, will stay undercover until we move on. If he thinks we're stayin' put behind those walls and not taking him any further to the hole-up, he'll send his boys in for us, sneaky like and us and our *amigos* will find ourselves locked in a snipin' war. And we ain't got the water to partake in a long fight in this sun.'

'Give me a few minutes, pard,' Blaze said, 'and I'll stir up those Slash Y boys somewhat. Enough I reckon to have them to go chargin' at that hut. You just keep strollin' along, Mr Larribee, but you oughta be prepared to move fast when I come back.'

Before Larribee could ask Blaze what he was planning to do, he had slipped into the undergrowth and out of his sight without so much as shaking a branch.

Larribee finished buttoning up his flies and walked across what he had promised his Mexican *compadres* would be the killing field.

★ ★ ★

'Where's the kid gone, Lacey?' an anxious-voiced Cal asked. 'If we've lost him Simpson will have my balls!'

The pair, screened by the brush, saw that the kid's partner was walking on his own.

'We ain't lost him, Cal,' replied Lacey. 'He's probably been taken short. Anyway we can't do damn all about it;

if we step out his partner will spot us and we'll both have to hold on to our balls!'

Lacey was more uneasy about the kid's vanishing act than he had let on to Cal. The kid for some reason or other was shooting down Slash Y men, his buddies, and he didn't want the son-of-a-bitch roaming around where he couldn't see him.

There came a slight rustling behind them and Cal swung round. The unexpected sight of the evil-smiling kid standing facing him, froze Cal's life-preserving instincts for a split second of time. Horrified-eyed he saw the kid's pistol flame, heard its crack, then felt a flash of extreme agony and was dead before he hit the dirt. Lacey did have the time to swing his rifle round but the thick brush hampered his frantic effort and Blaze's second load put another eye in his forehead before he could pull off a shot, dropping him to the ground as dead as Cal.

Simpson and his men stopped dead

in their tracks, hands nervously raising rifles, on hearing the two shots. Some uncanny inner feeling told Simpson that it wasn't Cal, who, despite his order, had sought revenge and fired the shots. He steeled himself to discover that two more of his crew were dead. And the hot trail to the raiders' camp lost.

Simpson heard the angry muttering and dirty-mouthing of his crew when they came across the two sprawled bodies. He looked down at them dispassionately and opined that they must have accidentally shown themselves to the sharp-eyed men they were tracking and paid the ultimate price for their carelessness. He pushed aside a branch and saw a long stretch of sloping open ground and, just where the ground began to climb again, the broken-down remains of a hut. Simpson's face lost some of its sourness. He hadn't lost his quarry just yet. They'd be keeping low behind what remained of the walls of that shack all set to make a hold back stand. When he led his men out into the clear the bastards would lay down a hail of rifle fire forcing them to scatter and seek cover before they could fire back. That would win them the few minutes it would take for them to cut and run for it over ground where they couldn't be tracked. Simpson looked about him to pick out the best approaches to the shack to allow his men to sneak in under cover and box in the raiders. It annoyed him somewhat that he wouldn't be stringing up the Mexican boys, but he reckoned that without their *gringo compadres* they would soon get careless, like Cal and Lacey had, and fall into his crew's hands. But first Cal and Lacey had to be buried, but quickly, he was impatient to draw blood.

'They ain't chargin' yet, Blaze,' grumbled a still panting Larribee after their mad dash to the shack when Blaze had rejoined him.

'They will,' Blaze replied. 'You can see by all the to and froin' goin' on in that undergrowth Simpson and the rest of his men are there.' He grinned at the glum-faced Larribee. 'They just need a mite more chivvying up that's all. I know that they're a bunch of bullying, stompin' men but they've pride of a sort. They're not used to see their *compadres* shot down and unable to do anything about it. They're the *hombres* who generally do the shootin' and they won't be likin' it.'

Blaze looked at the tensed-faced Villa and the rest of the small army. 'Just hang-fire a while, *amigos*,' he said, 'until I rile those fellas a mite more,' and brought his rifle up to his shoulder.

Simpson and his men flung themselves belly down to the ground as the full fifteen-shot load of Winchester magazine scythed through the brush. Jack and Sancho, not quick enough to hug the dirt, gave out with sharp cries of pain and curses as they were hit. It was painful enough for Sancho to wish that when Bull had been killed he should have carried on riding north to let Simpson fight his own battles.

Butler, a top hand, was the first to get to his feet after the firing had stopped. He gimlet-eyed Simpson.

'I don't know what plan you're thinkin' of so we can flush out those bastards, boss,' he said. 'But I ain't lyin' eatin' dirt just to end up like Cal and Lacey. I'm all for goin' at them shootin'. There's only two of them. If we go in fast and well spread out we'll be among them before they can reload.'

Before Simpson could say he had a less risky way to tackle the two raiders, all his crew were standing up, even Jack and Sancho who were showing leg wounds. And Simpson thought that he had seen kinder-looking wolf packs. He couldn't hold them back.

'OK, boys,' he said. 'Let's go and take them!'

'Wait, *amigos*, wait,' Larribee said, as the line of hollering men burst into the open. 'Let me and Blaze fire a few rounds at them just to keep them believin' there's only a couple of us here. We don't want to go off at half-cock and show our aces until they're close enough not to miss puttin' them down.' He had to take in account that his Mexican *compadres* weren't crack-shots like Blaze. Even he was only a fair shot compared to the kid.

The Slash Y men kept up their blood-mad rush, running in a curved extended line, the flank men speeding to close in on the rear of the shack to cut off the escape route of the men they were eager to hang. Two of them stopped to pull off a shot at the shack, their *compadres* wanting to get within easy rifle range before dropping to the ground and blasting the raiders out of the shack with their concentrated fire.

A snap shot from Larribee put Sancho beyond any more wishful thoughts this side of hell and Blaze sent his target, Jack, crashing to the ground. Then Larribee judged that it was the killing time. He nodded to Villa and the impatient waiting jaws reached up and laid their rifles across the wall and took aim.

A roaring wall of flame swept along the front of the shack and the Slash Y men, with cries and groans, wilted and fell under the hail of lead. The two ranch hands who were still standing made to turn and run back to the shelter of the brush. The second fusillade killed them several times over.

'OK, *amigos*!' Larribee shouted. 'It's all over!' He swallowed hard. He had seen much fearful carnage during the war but the sight of nine, ten men, killed in a matter of seconds still upset him.

Through the thick acrid gunsmoke he eyed the three brothers and saw in their eyes what they must be feeling inside. Which was all to the good, he thought; they weren't getting a liking for killing. They weren't destined for the lawless trail like Blaze, and him.

'Good work, *compadres*,' he said addressing them all. 'Now let's go and check on them. One or two could need our help; the rest we'll have to bury in the nearest wash. But keep on the alert. A wounded man, if he's conscious, will want to get even with the *hombre* who's causin' him all his pain.'

They picked their way among the bodies stretched out in violent patterns of death, Larribee coming across the dead Simpson lying spreadeagled, his back against a hump in the ground. His duster was wide open and Larribee saw the growing dark stain on the front of his fancy white shirt. Close by his right hand lay a long-barrelled Colt Dragoon pistol. The dead rancher didn't seem any bigger built than the Mexican boys, he thought, yet his big, high and mighty pride, had got him and a bunch of his men killed. He moved away from Simpson to check out another body when he heard Blaze yell, 'Look out!'

As Larribee swung round he swore that he felt the heat of Blaze's shot as it zipped close by him. He now saw another growing stain on Simpson's shirt. He was dead for real this time, but his right hand still gripped hold of the Dragoon. 'It's the first time I've been thrown down on by a dead man, Blaze,' he said shakily.

Blaze grinned at him. 'An old *hombre* once told me that if you start a gunfight make sure you finish it.'

'Yeah, well, m'be,' a still shaken irritable Larribee snapped. Then he quickly, and silently, cursed himself for allowing his tetchy nerves to get the better of him. The kid had saved his life and paid off the debt he reckoned he owed him. He didn't deserve to be snarled at. In a more normal tone he said, 'Now let's start gettin' these bodies down into the nearest wash and covered up with stones. We ain't got the gear to give them a real burial before some rider passes by, and then we'd have a whole heap of explainin' to do.'

16

The six *compadres* were sitting at the fire having their last mugs of coffee together. Villa and his grandsons had parcelled up their few belongings and now that the threat from the Slash Y was gone they were intending to return to their strip of land just north of the Mexican border and begin raising sheep again. Tomas was already on his way to La Paz to tell Carla that it was safe for her to return to the *hacienda*.

'I'm sorry you are breaking camp, *Señor* Villa,' he had said, as he was mounting his mule. 'I may be passing by this way again, with the *hacienda's* wagon loaded with Señor Brewster and the *señorita's* belongings. I heard Señora Sofia say that the *señor* was thinking of setting up his business in La Paz.' Tomas grinned. 'I shall miss your fine *gringo* coffee, *amigo*.'

Larribee had noticed that since Tomas had ridden out Blaze hadn't said much. He was answering the brothers' questions with a curt, '*Si*' or '*Nada*'. His partner had something nagging at him, Larribee thought. Had he got religion and regretted the shooting of the Slash Y men? Or was he doing some deep thinking of where he should head for, now their partnership had ended with the death of Simpson? Whatever, it was the kid's business not his.

Blaze's asking Villa if he had thought of raising cattle instead of sheep had Larribee, in spite of him not wanting to poke his nose into his former partner's affairs, raising a puzzled eyebrow.

Villa laughed. 'I am not a rich don, Señor Blaze, with plenty of *dinero* to buy expensive longhorns.'

'I know where there's nigh on two hundred head of cattle, Señor Villa,' replied Blaze. 'Well fed, peaceful and calm like, that even a coupla *gringo bandidos* and four Mexican sheepherders could get them on to their feet and herd them all the way to Mexico. If you know of a good stretch of open range thereabouts with grass and water, we could build us a real cattle spread. We'd all be equal partners.' Blaze gave a grin. 'They happen to be the late Mr Simpson's cows, but finders keepers I reckon. We can brand them with our own mark.'

'I know such a place, rancher Blaze,' Villa said, straight-faced. 'And I can get you three hard-working *vaqueros*.'

'*Bueno!*' said Blaze, then looked at Larribee. 'How does bein' a cattleman sit with you, Mr Larribee?'

Larribee gave an inner smile. He knew now what had been chewing away at the kid: female business. 'I had a hankerin' to be a rancher after I robbed my next bank but events kinda overwhelmed me. I'm in, on one condition.' Then he added, po-faced, 'That one of the equal partners in this enterprise pulls his equal weight and don't miss out on his chores by payin' too many calls on a certain *señorita* who could happen to be livin' close by.'

'It ain't like that at all!' Blaze spluttered, his face colouring up.

'Like hell it ain't!' Larribee growled. Then, grinning, he said, 'You're in with a chance, boy. What *señorita* could resist the charms of an up-and-comin' *gringo* cattle baron?' And soberly thought that sparking up to a girl, successful or not, was a damn sight less dangerous pastime than riding with the death shadow at your side.

Blaze stood up and kicked dirt on the fire. 'Come on you apologies for *vaqueros*,' he mock-growled. 'We've got some beef to move!'

Five grinning *vaqueros* threw their coffee dregs on the smoking fire and got to their feet.

THE END

We do hope that you have enjoyed reading this large print book.

Did you know that all of our titles are available for purchase?

We publish a wide range of high quality large print books including:
Romances, Mysteries, Classics
General Fiction
Non Fiction and Westerns

Special interest titles available in large print are:
The Little Oxford Dictionary
Music Book, Song Book
Hymn Book, Service Book

Also available from us courtesy of Oxford University Press:
Young Readers' Dictionary
(large print edition)
Young Readers' Thesaurus
(large print edition)

For further information or a free brochure, please contact us at:
Ulverscroft Large Print Books Ltd.,
The Green, Bradgate Road, Anstey,
Leicester, LE7 7FU, England.
Tel: (00 44) **0116 236 4325**
Fax: (00 44) **0116 234 0205**

Other titles in the
Linford Western Library:

JUST BREATHIN' HATE

Dempsey Clay

When the Law went loco and charged him with killing his wife, innocent Jack Fallon had two choices only — run or hang. So he ran — to a strange lost valley shut off from the world and ruled by a cult of holy men who would prove more lethal than any posse could ever be . . .

THE FENCE BUSTERS

Tom Gordon

The open Texas range was the finest cattle-land in the world. But when some forward thinking men erected fences, others suffered the consequences as their cattle were deprived of water and the best grassland. These men turned night-riders, destroying the long fence lines. Lives were lost and property ruined ... Young and reckless, Tom Midnight joined the ranks of the fencers; his flaming guns were there to argue with the eastern speculators, seeking to fan the flames of conflict.

DELUGE!

Arnold Ryden

When Jeff Alroyd rides into a divided valley, he discovers that the Circle C Ranch, owned by Babs Kemp and her father, is under threat because adjoining landowner 'Poker' Barrow has sabotaged their stream. Jeff Alroyd is determined to help Babs by using his expertise as a mining engineer and poker player. Jeff outwits Barrow and regains the stolen water, but when Barrow resorts to murder and kidnapping, Jeff finds himself apparently beaten — without money, pipeline or water.